FENELLA, A WITCH

THE DRIFTLESS UNSOLICITED NOVELLA SERIES

Technologies of the Self	Haris A. Durrani
Faith Healer	Victoria G. Smith
Girling	C. Kubasta
Rosa	Barbara de la Cuesta
Fenella, A Witch	Stefanie Moers
Ivywood Manor	Tani Loo
The Meadow	Mihka Emani

THE DRIFTLESS UNSOLICITED NOVELLA SERIES

FENELLA, A WITCH

STEFANIE MOERS

BRAIN MILL PRESS
GREEN BAY, WISCONSIN

Published in the United States by Brain Mill Press.
Print ISBN 978-1-948559-37-9
EPUB ISBN 978-1-948559-40-9
MOBI ISBN 978-1-948559-38-6
PDF ISBN 978-1-948559-39-3

Cover design by Ampersand Book Design.

www.brainmillpress.com

Published by Brain Mill Press, the Driftless Unsolicited Novella Series publishes those novellas selected as winners of the Driftless Unsolicited Novella Contest each year.

FOR DAVID

FENELLA, A WITCH

The morning after doing the murder, Fenella looks out her window, trying to think of a better place to put the head. It can't be buried with his body because that would mean confessing, and Fenella isn't stupid enough to do such a thing. She crosses her arms and continues looking out the window and uncrosses her arms and takes a drink of milk. She doesn't feel bad at all, or worried. She feels a little guilty because she's told her lawyer friend about doing it and she knows she shouldn't have told anyone. *Well, I won't tell anyone else*, she thinks and walks away from the window.

She stands in her dining room, underneath the pale pink ceiling painted with ladies in black gowns. She looks up at them, her ladies.

"Oh ladies," she says. "I can wear black now too. You needn't look down upon me anymore." She laughs and goes into the kitchen to put the empty milk glass into the sink.

After her bath, during which she gazes at the ceiling and thinks the black-clad ladies would look nice floating up there, too, she gets dressed in a slim black cashmere sweater and a voluminous black pleated skirt and drives to the grocery store, leaving the bagged-up head in her freezer behind the Neapolitan ice cream.

At the grocery store, she fills a cart with necessaries: toilet paper, toothpaste, coffee, milk. While the cashier scans her purchases, Fenella flicks through the pages of the little black notebook she uses to hold her credit card and license until she comes to the page where she has written out the grocery list; with her little golden pen, she slashes over the items on the list and writes down the day's date. Fenella writes down everything she wants in her little black notebook, and when she gets it, she crosses it out and makes a note of the date. She says no to the bag boy asking if she needs her bag carried out to her car and takes her receipt.

When she gets home, she goes back to bed. *Why did I do this*? she asks herself. *What was I hoping to accomplish? Why have I forgotten so soon? What did I mean to change?* She can't remember what she was thinking, or what she was like yesterday. She can't remember why she had wanted to do it. It had something to do with finding out something about herself, but now that seems so silly. She has done something so bad and there isn't even enough herself to feel bad about doing it.

She has a feeling she has been lost for a long time in dark woods, looking for something. Now all the trees around her have been cut down, and she need only walk right toward the center. But what is at the center? What had she meant to find there?

Soon she falls asleep and sleeps for a long, long time.

Fenella wakes up lying in a fetal position. She rolls over and watches the ceiling for a little while. In her dream, she was on the ceiling looking down at herself. Fenella likes her dreams. She remembers them as a series of fashion plates telling a great story. Her dreams are much more interesting than her life.

In her sleep, she has cupped her arm under her head to keep the post of an earring from digging into her scalp, and now her arm is asleep and tingling. She shakes it and waits for the feeling to come back to her fingers. She wiggles her fingers and waits, she thinks about her dream. When her arm is awake, she gets out of bed.

Fenella isn't a morning person. She doesn't remember language until she has been awake for at least an hour, and she doesn't try to be nice. She stands at the foot of her bed and straightens the covers, looking around, frowning. Her room is bare-walled and dusty. The walls are bone white and the curtains are frothy and black. The floor is hardwood and there's a large stain on the ceiling above the window from a roof leak. It took Fenella forever to tell the landlord about the leak because she dislikes strangers creeping about her apartment while she's gone.

She goes into the bathroom and closes the door and looks at herself in the mirror from the shoulders up while the bathwater runs. She tests the temperature and drips oil into the tub. A good smell. The water stops being clear and turns ghost white. She removes her earrings and gets in the tub. She goes all the way under and comes up and rests her head on the back of the tub and drapes her arms along the sides and closes her eyes and breathes in the steam. After a while, she shampoos her hair, runs her razor over her legs, and gets out of the tub.

Before her skin is completely dry, she rubs French lavender-and-milk lotion all over herself. At the sink, she washes her face and dries it and rubs an illuminating moisturizer into her cheekbones. She puts powder foundation under her eyes and on her nose and uses her little finger to dip into the pot of shimmering pink eye shadow and applies it to the inner corner of her eyes. Her hair is straight and thick to her waist so she blow-dries the top smooth and glossy and combs the rest out with her fingers; she'll let it dry by itself.

She puts in her earrings again and goes into her bedroom to get dressed. She takes a pair of underwear out of the top dresser drawer and steps into them. So simple compared with the underwear of the past decades. Fenella most likes the crotchless bloomers of the nineteenth century and wonders if the fine ladies walking about so exposed beneath all their other layers thought their underwear was so simple too. She opens the closet. She has white shirts and black, and black dresses and some trousers. The overhead light is poor quality. She flicks it off, shuts the door, and goes back to the dresser. In the bottom drawer, she finds her favorite black sweater. She pulls it over her head without bothering with a brassiere. She doesn't feel like putting on pants yet. Everywhere, everywhere she looks for her black ballet slippers and cannot find them. On her way to the kitchen, she finds them and puts them on.

In the kitchen, she peels a hard-boiled egg and makes coffee and waters her dying lavender plants. She presses a sprig between her fingers to crush the scent out. It smells pure and clean, like morning. She nips a branch off with her fingernails and throws open some drawers, looking for a box of pins. When she finds it, she takes one out and pins the sprig to the neck of her sweater for a blouse brooch. The coffee finishes brewing; she drinks a cup of it, black. She doesn't feel right.

A bus or a garbage truck drives by and the building vibrates. The vibrations set off the music box on Fenella's dresser, a unicorn on a carousel post in front of a castle, and the few notes of tinkling carnival music wake Fenella up. Fenella, too, vibrates with energy all through her body. This will be a terrible day until she calms down. She must do something boring and detailed to achieve that goal. She gets out of bed. She slept in a pair of control top black La Perla underwear with lines of ivory stitches fanned up over the waist, and nothing else.

She stretches her arms over her head and yawns and puts black ballet slippers on her feet. Yesterday's sweater is on the floor. She picks it up and puts it on, cuddling happily into it as it touches her skin. She's cold! The heaters in her building get turned off in April but the mornings are still cold, and Fenella sleeps with the windows open; she loves fresh air. It's the in-between, uncomfortable time; she sleeps naked because she gets hot, the temperature drops overnight, and she wakes up in a cold sweat. Her sheets are never the perfect nest they are in summer, when the air is dry from air conditioning, and in the winter dry from the heat; in springtime, they are a tangled mass of dampness. If Fenella were a plant, her bed would be the perfect garden to grow in.

She walks through her apartment, keeping her arms out of the sleeves of the sweater; she hugs herself underneath the sweater and the sleeves stick out like amputee stumps. Her breasts are cold, she can feel her nipples pressing against the back of her arms, she wants them to go down, but the rest of her skin is covered in goose bumps too.

Being cold is a spare feeling. When Fenella was young, she had a friend who lived in an old farmhouse. On the top floor, there was a spare room called the Cold Room. When they played haunted house or secret passage, that room was always the bad one. This morning, Fenella feels like her body is that room, uncomfortable and forgotten; her mind is trying to leap out of it.

In the kitchen, she puts her right arm properly through the sweater sleeve and turns the knob on the gas stove. Blue flames leap up in a ring under their black iron corona. It's a gas stovc; shc could kill hcrsclf if shc likes. She warms her hand instead, then fills the teapot with water from the tap and puts it on top of the stove.

As she waits for it to boil, she looks into her freezer. The black bag of head is taking up a lot of room. It isn't a very large freezer. She puts her left arm through its sleeve and reaches into the freezer and pushes the bag back a little bit. Upset from its sturdy perch, the bag falls forward. Fenella catches it with both hands before it falls on its face and carefully props it against the back wall of the freezer. She moves the carton of ice cream beside it for support.

Then suddenly, she is hot, sweating, the same way she feels when she is caught speeding and gets pulled over for a ticket. Fenella, always amazed when her brain reacts in a primordial way to something she does that she thinks nothing of doing, stands still to catch her breath. What do those millennially old patterns know of the modern Fenella that she does not know herself?

Everything, says the omniscient god within herself, the ancient brain, the amygdala; it knows everything she does not, she cannot purge it. And what then is this Fenella creature walking through the steps of making tea, in a hand-knit sweater she thought herself clever for making, but a preposterous joke? *Look at the little creature*, the ancient brain says, *thinking she is so smart. I know better*, it tells her, and Fenella laughs out loud, exuberant, she has no idea, then, who or what on this earth she is.

THIS MORNING, THERE IS A MEMORIAL SERVICE FOR HIM. FENELLA ONLY KNOWS ABOUT IT BECAUSE SHE READS IT IN THE NEWSPAPER VERY EARLY WHILE she drinks coffee under her lady ceiling. The black table and chairs are antiques and creak whenever she moves. It's an annoying noise and she tries to stay still.

She reads a few sentences of the newspaper story and stops. She's remembered her dream. She's dreamed of sex. She was in her bathtub in deep warm water and she was struggling to wake up. There was some sort of sedation in her brain she struggled to get around. There was pain that was both external and within her, and it was him, he was having intercourse with her. She put her hand down to check if he was inside of her. She was having a very hard time telling for certain. He was. Why should it be so hard to tell what someone is doing with her? She turned her head and saw smears of blood on the side of the tub.

She closes her eyes and sees it all again, a visceral memory that occurred in no time but her own. Is this what will happen when she sleeps now? Like the handing over of an apartment key at the end of the lease, who will move into her, what will she be? She wants only to be alone. Solo, sole Fenella, stepping dripping out of a bath and into black shoes. All alone. It's safer, it's better. She's through with all the other things. They take her to too-dark places. But these things come over her sometimes.

Fenella looks back down at the newspaper. The story was never a headline story; it was on the bottom of the front page first and since then has been relegated to the metropolitan section. She reads a few more sentences of the story. He has two sisters, she never knew that. *Well*, she supposes, *he doesn't know I have sisters, so why should I know he has sisters?* She herself has two sisters and thinks it's strange when other people don't have two sisters. Two sisters is the natural way of things. One sister says of her brother, "He was a good person, very sweet."

There are no pictures of the sisters. Fenella imagines his sisters as being beautiful and intelligent and wearing great clothes. She is always intimidated by people she doesn't know and only hears of. When she only hears of someone, she always thinks they must be more beautiful and smarter than her, and so she automatically dislikes them.

There are other people in the world who know him better than me, she thinks, and this breaks down her dream and resolve. Fenella would like very much to go to the memorial service and meet his sisters. They can talk about their brother with Fenella and share amusing anecdotes.

Fenella looks up at her black-dressed ladies and considers. She daydreams. In the way of daydreams, she has no corporeal self, it is just her mind floating about, watching the two sisters as they hover and converse and are lovely and mournful, they look at Fenella as Fenella writes her name in the guest book, they try to place her, they cannot, later they are reading the names and they come to Fenella's; they look at each other, they think, one says, "Fenella?" The other answers, "Fenella…I don't think…oh wait…she was that girl," "Yes, that girl he was in love with," "Her name was Fenella? He never told me her name," "It was Fenella, he loved her, he loved her, I wonder why he never said anything about her."

WHEN FENELLA WAS A LITTLE GIRL, SHE HAD RECURRING BAD DREAMS. ONE SET WAS ABOUT TORNADOES, BUT EVEN BEFORE THOSE BEGAN, SHE would dream of giant bad birds flying over her house. She would be in the dreams with her mother. They would be doing something pleasant and then Fenella's mother would start knowing that the birds were coming, and she and Fenella would have to hide. Usually they went under the bed and waited for the birds to fly over. There were two birds and they couldn't know anyone was in the house or they would do bad things. Fenella could feel it as the birds flew over the house, in probably the same way her mother sensed that they were coming.

Now she lies in bed at dawn and tries to feel if any birds are flying over her apartment. She should be able to feel it, she is on the top floor. She concentrates. She wonders if she will ever appear in someone's dream as a mother. If she ever has a daughter, she would like to pass this dream on to her. Fenella will be the mother in it, of course. Her lovely little daughter! They will be writing stories together at the kitchen table and Fenella will get the warning feeling. Her daughter will have on a dress. Fenella only ever wore dresses when she was little. Her daughter will too. Fenella will wear a more grown-up version of her daughter's dress. Fenella will snatch her little daughter's hand and they will whirl into the bedroom in their similar dresses and creep underneath the bed together, holding hands and waiting for the danger to pass.

Once, in one of her dreams, Fenella crawled out from under the bed and crept along the wall until she could peek out the window. She saw the specks of the huge dark birds flying off, and she was terrified because seeing them meant they were real. She had never seen them before and supposed that her mother was making it all up.

Fenella will let her little daughter see the birds immediately, in the first dream, because she wants her daughter to believe her thoroughly. Believing in someone thoroughly is a beautiful pure thing. Everything about Fenella and her daughter will be beautiful and pure. Fenella will teach her that when she feels something, it is real. Feelings make things real. Without feelings, the world would be a cold dead place, full of beautiful, pointless things.

But Fenella can't feel any birds. She misses having her mother in her dreams. She hasn't dreamed about her mother in as long as she can remember. Dreaming of people puts a sort of special polish onto their real selves, especially mothers.

Fenella wishes she had become pregnant before she killed him. Everyone with babies seems so happy, they don't have to think about anything else anymore. She wonders, *what is it like to not think of anything else*? He would have made a beautiful little girl with dark eyes, pink cat mouth, Fenella's sharp nose and high cheekbones. Now she must find someone else who can make her pregnant if that's what she decides to do. It's such a hassle.

She wonders if she could harness all the energy in the world and make it put a child into her. She can have a little witch child. For now, there is dismal chance of immaculate conception because she can't even feel a bird flying over her head. *Sensing birds*, Fenella thinks, *is a natural precursor to being able to summon a child into existence.* She will work on it. And in the sleeping mind of her little daughter, they will spin together out of the kitchen and under the bed and hide from the large malevolent birds who mean them so much harm. Fenella rolls over onto her stomach and goes back to sleep, feeling much more serene now that she has a plan.

FENELLA DRAGS HERSELF OUT OF BED AND GETS DRESSED IN A BLACK LEOTARD AND BLACK SWEATPANTS WITH A DRAWSTRING WAIST. SHE PUTS black canvas ballet slippers into her purse and puts her feet into black Converse. She stands in front of the bathroom mirror and pushes her hair out of her face with a piece of thin elastic, she considers her face, she thinks she would look good with a shaved head. She would have to wear more makeup.

She goes to the kitchen, waters her lavender, and buries her face in it for a moment, letting it brush and tingle against her cheeks, then she exits her apartment and walks downtown toward the Clairn Dance School where she works out.

When she gets to the Clairn, she goes inside, gets her card punched, buys a bottle of water, and goes up to the third floor. Her class is in studio six. Fenella goes inside and dumps her purse against the wall and sits down to change her shoes.

She catches the teacher's eye, a young woman who always wears black leggings and looks at Fenella with suspicion, and looks away. This is a gentle free-form movement class with classical ballet infusion for pregnant women and for mothers and young daughters. It's Fenella's favorite class. When the teacher starts class, Fenella keeps to the back of the room.

"All right, everyone," the young woman in black leggings says, "let's warm up."

The little girls move toward the front of the room and watch her eagerly. Fenella smiles, it's sweet to see her fans. The teacher brings her hands up into the air, flattens her palms out over her head, and says, "And what do we say about the ground?" and all the little girls throw their hands up in the air and say back, "The ground is not just a place to put your feet!" and the teacher and the girls all stretch downwards and put their hands on their feet and their noses against their knees.

Fenella starts to get light-headed and she lifts her head earlier than anyone else. The pianist in the back corner begins to tinkle out a few notes as the young woman in black leggings leads everyone through stretching movements. "Time for flowers," she says finally. This is the last warm-up. Fenella is seated, stretching out her calves, and she draws her knees up to her forehead in imitation.

"Imagine you are a flower seed, buried in the dirt." Fenella imagines herself as a lavender seedling.

"Feel the dirt around you, holding you tight, everything is dark. Now feel yourself grow as the dirt turns damp, you can feel something you've never felt before, it's sunlight, it draws you upward, you go upward as gracefully as you can," and everyone very slowly uncurls and lifts up their arms slowly, deliberately, "but once that sunlight hits you, you POP," and everyone except the pregnant women jumps up to her feet, "and you begin to expand."

The energy in the room turns more powerful as everyone imagines themselves expanding. Fenella sprouts several more branchcs.

"You put out delicate blossoms. You have a natural fragrance." The divinity comes upon Fenella and blesses her.

"You move with the air." Fenella can feel the air turning her head, carrying her scent.

"And then something terrible happens. You get CUT!" and everyone plops with melodramatic aplomb to the ground again as the pianist hits a loud trilling minor chord. The pregnant women lower themselves gently. Fenella lies prone on the ground. She is dead. The little girls lie on the ground in their fuzzy sweaters and frothy tutus, laughing hysterically. The mothers and mothers-to-be look at one another and smile knowingly. Fenella casts aside her dead branches and prepares to dance as the pianist begins playing something classical. Even Fenella's dead branches smell sweet.

WITCHES ARE FASCINATING, THEY ALWAYS HAVE BEEN. IN THE CHILDREN'S SECTION OF THE LIBRARY, FENELLA SITS CROSS-LEGGED ON THE floor in front of a row of witch books, wearing a crown of lavender branches on her head and a black cambric shirtdress with about eight yards of fabric in the skirt and a row of heart-shaped mother-of-pearl buttons buttoned all the way up the bodice. The collar is very pointy, the points point down at her breasts, she has put collar stays in the collar edges to keep them perfect and flat.

She drinks from a take-out cup of milky green tea and reads a book called *Witch's Sister*, fully absorbed in it. After taking a sip of tea, she sets it on the ground beside her, upon the fabric of her skirt, or she puts it on the bookshelf in front of her; she turns a page and licks her lips and reads on. This was one of her favorite series of books when she was a little girl. They taught her everything she knows about witches, that they are glamorous to young girls, they are wicked, they are indomitable, and they like herbs.

When she worked for the library, she despised people who sat in the aisles and blocked the way, but now, as a mother and her young daughter hover around the aisle edge, Fenella ignores them. She is one of them now, she is a patron, she doesn't have to move for anything if she doesn't want to.

The mother and the daughter whisper and consult each other, maybe they want the shelf of books above

Fenella's head, neither are brave or rude enough to attempt it. Fenella is peripherally aware of this as she drinks her tea and reads; they are distracting her from her concentration, and because of this, she is pleased to be causing them an obstacle. She is aware when they move off and when they come back with a librarian. The librarian steps right on Fenella's skirt as she reaches over Fenella's head for the book the young girl wants. The shoe of the librarian is black and dull. Fenella thinks, *She did that on purpose.*

"Oops, don't mind me," the librarian says to Fenella. "There you go," she says to the young girl and hands her the book.

"Say thank you," says the mother to her daughter, and the mother says "Thank you" to the librarian and the daughter says, "Thank you" too and they all leave Fenella to read in peace.

Fenella brushes the shoe print from the librarian's shoe off her black skirt. She reads on. She is mouthing the words of the book's song to herself when a sensation thrills through her. Fenella turns her head sharply. A different little girl is standing there, very close, studying her. She is three or four years old. It was the sound of her breath Fenella heard.

"What's on your head?" the little girl asks. She has a lovely, pure, husky voice.

"A crown," Fenella says.

"It doesn't look like my crown," the little girl tells her in that dark, wonderful, adult-sounding voice.

"Your crown is probably polyethylene and made in China by a very poor little girl," Fenella tells her, full of scorn. Fenella's is real. It will live, it will die. She's jealous of the little girl's lovely voice, it will give her good advantage in life. The girl sticks out her tongue and turns and skips off.

Fenella looks back down at the book in her lap but her concentration is broken. Her hand is pale in her dark skirt, the pages of the book are darker than her skin. She can't read here anymore. The whole area now is full of the sound of high young sweet voices of children, the laughter and scolding of mothers. It's storytime. Fenella pushes the row of witch books from the shelf into her full skirt and picks up her cup and gathers the hem of her skirt into her fist and stands up and goes to check out.

SHE WAS CLEANING HER CLOSET BUT NOW SHE SIMPLY FLOATS IN A SEA OF BLACK FLATS. THE BACK WALL IS BRICKED WITH SHOE BOXES HALFWAY UP, some boxes fatter than others, some red and some pale brown, those are her French and Italian high heels. She is thoroughly tired of them, their day is done. Their day was one of confection and whimsy. Now Fenella wants only things that are plain and serious like her black flats. Facts are a dull glamour but they are pure, unlike daydreams, those have no boundaries. She is taking all the black flats out of their narrow boxes and cataloguing them for her own pleasure in her little black book.

She has so many pairs of black flats! So many of them unworn. She needs to start wearing them. They are all the same, they are all black flats, but they are all different too. It is the greatest, sweetest pleasure to walk for a coffee in a pair of black flats.

She pulls a box into her lap and opens it. This is a pair of black patent leather flats. She can only remember wearing these a few times. The inside is soft pink suede and the soles are pale fawn suede with a little bit of scuffing. In her black notebook, opened on the floor beside her, she writes, *Black patent flats* and puts the pen into the spine of the notebook to mark her place. Then she uncrosses her legs, tries the shoes on, and admires them.

Randomly she selects another box and takes it out of the stack. She opens it up. The flats in this box are in an organza bag. Fenella pulls at the tied ribbon and loosens it and spills the shoes out into her lap. Black leather, with a black leather toe cap. Putting the shoes on her hands and flipping them over she inspects the soles: no scuffing. She writes: *Black leather with black toe cap*. All of these black flats have elastic cords running through the edges so a lady can tie a bow in front and fit the shoe to hug her foot. Fenella takes off her right black patent flat and replaces it with the black-on-black. She flexes her foot. *Why have I never worn these?* she thinks. The black on black is an intense combination.

A moody, haughty subtlety like greeting a person with merely a nod.

Out of the stacks comes another box. In this one is Fenella's extra pair of her daily black flats, saved for when the soles run out on her current pair. Her sweetest favorites, they are perfect. She writes, *Classic black, elastic bow, slightly pearly*. She thinks she has another pair of these somewhere in the closet, also unworn. There was a period of time when this shoe was not being manufactured and Fenella had to contact the company directly to order dead stock in her size. She is very dependent on this shoe; it takes her everywhere. When she found out she could no longer order it, she was very depressed, and then remembered she could pull strings maybe because she was rich. It worked. She doesn't know what she will do when these three pairs run out, she will probably die. *It will be a good reason to finally commit suicide*, she thinks. All hope gone.

Next to *Classic black, elastic bow, slightly pearly*, she draws a bad skull and crossbones.

She wraps this pair back up in the white tissue paper and puts the box back into the stack. On an afterthought, she draws a little star on the box so if her apartment catches fire, she will know what shoe box to take.

The next pair is luxurious, gleaming soft and thin black leather with squared toes like the dance teacher's pointe shoes. Fenella writes *Square toes*. She hasn't worn these yet either. They are the ones she wanted the most.

They are the most expensive of her black flat collection, and since Fenella is a penny pincher at heart, she waited for a long, long time to buy them, and she filled all that time with dreaming of them. Now they are in her closet, pickling nicely; they have all been sold out.

When she was waiting and planning to buy them, she thought about them very often; they were very special; now she has them, there is nothing special about them, they are just another thing she has. It would have been better to let them sell out. She strokes the leather with her index finger. *No*, she thinks, *I am glad*. She holds the shoe against her cheek. The leather is cool and unloving.

Her tea this morning is Earl Grey with milk. Slouching, she stands beneath her dark ladies, looking around the room. She sees new shadows everywhere. They cast new shadows for her now. The ceiling panels they're painted on are from an old building downtown that's being gutted and re-turned into a hotel. First it was a hotel, pestered by a rash of suicides in the early twentieth century, then it was a bank, pestered by a black economy, and then it was going to be condominiums, and now it's going to be a hotel again.

Her left arm is crossed over her waist and her left hand is tucked underneath her right elbow, her teacup dangles lazy and heavy from the fingers of her right hand, with a little bit of lukewarm tea left in it. From the tip of her left index finger, the little tin tea bag sieve hangs, empty, the tea bag is still in her cup; her right index finger, held up and away from the cup handle, is hooked through the handle of the little tin cream pot that had had the milk in it. When she moves the cup to her mouth, the cream pot clanks against the cup and makes a noise.

She can do so many very simple things at a time without even thinking about them, it is amazing, it fascinates her as she stands in shadow thinking of them. She should start thinking of them, every time she does something, and be properly amazed. It will make life more interesting. She tucks her chin down and tilts the cup up and sips and thinks about doing it. Her nose makes a shadow in the tea.

Her feet are bare; she wears a black French boiled wool shift with pale crescent-shaped patch pockets underneath her breasts and a zipper up the back. She thinks about it. All shadowed.

Every now and then, she tilts her head back to look at the ceiling. The ladies gaze dully back down at her. There is nothing to say to them and they have nothing to say to her. They simply know each other, like sisters, and are tired of the other's redundancies. They will not speak just for the duty of it. *Hello, I am Fenella*, she thinks anyway, and for the fun of it, she begins to think out everything she is doing to fascinate herself further.

I have no shoes on. I am standing up. I am wearing a

black dress. My arms are crossed, I am holding a cup, a little cream pot, a tea bag strainer. I am looking at the floor, now the ceiling, because my eyes are open. I am breathing. My stomach is digesting tea, I don't even have to ask it to, it just does it on its own. My tongue is feeling my mouth. I can feel fabric against my skin. The first time I touched this fabric was on a fabric bolt, it was between black silk and black bouclé. I am thinking of what shoes to put on, I am thinking I want a drink of tea, I am moving my arm and I am opening my mouth and tea is going into my mouth and it is warm and creamy and down my throat and I am still barefoot, standing up. I am aware of everything around me.

How can she be standing still, doing nothing, when everything is occurring? Why should she have a need to do anything at all when standing in one place is so productive? It is so stupid, to do anything, a plant does nothing but grow, and a plant is full and whole and perfect, why should a mind do anything but think?

Doing, Fenella thinks, *is a side effect of thinking. Thinking something is never enough, but it should be*, she tells herself, *because thinking is the most amazing thing that can be done. How do we even do it?* she thinks, and yawns.

Special Collections in the old downtown library Athenaeum is the only place in Minnesota that has the book Fenella wants to read, so here she is, reading it. The book is called

Feathers in a Black Hat. At every point in her life, a book has found Fenella, a book that goes along with her life as it is at the moment. It is the divinity that follows her. Some people collect lovers as they carry on, others get money. For Fenella, a book always shines out of the murk. It's comforting to be provided with a new favorite and important book whenever she needs one.

The book found her like this: last night, a centipede was on the wall of her bedroom near the upper corner; she threw a magazine up at it to kill it. When the magazine fell, along with the wiggling long legs of the centipede, it was open to a page about a function that had been held at some theater. There were people pictured, smiling and holding cups of pink wine in front of a large painting of a pale woman on a pedestal wearing a Grecian black dress. Fenella liked the picture and spent a long time finding out who it was: it was a painting of the obscure and long-forgotten St. Paul moonshine-era writer Margot Bean. Fenella had never even heard of her. Her book doesn't seem to exist anymore, except here in Special Collections.

From what Fenella has read so far, *Feathers in a Black Hat* seems to be about a young woman falling into witchcraft and rejecting her posh Summit Avenue lifestyle. 'In the corner of the dim room, Estee sat on the pink footstool, waiting. The strings of black beads on her dress drooped to her ankles. She watched, in the well-lit corner, the diamonds sparkling. The pastel, sweet confections on the tables. Slim, pale necks outstretched as faces moved and conversed. A smell of singed feathers smoked the room as someone's hat nudged a candle.'

To be questioned, Fenella wears best black. She's actually pleased to be asked in, it means that maybe she has really done this thing. She wears a bouclé suit with a matching dark silk blouse that has an irritating wrinkle across the back and black flats and carries a wilting leather bag that was once upon a time her mother's.

She has never been in a police station before except once when her car was mistakenly towed, and she had to go complain and find out where it had been taken. This is a different station and the conference room she's in is small and has a window overlooking the back parking lot. The window is tinted and the view is tinged a rusty color. She takes a drink of her police station coffee, in a foam cup, mixed with nondairy creamer. She promises herself a cup of French roast after this, mixed with real cream, to be drunk in bed with a book.

She looks out the window. A crow has alighted into the branches of a tree out there beyond the parking lot. It perches midway up the crown, near the trunk, and caws so loudly she can hear it. Another crow flutters into the tree and lands a few branches below the first. They ignore each other, but they must know each other.

Fenella can't imagine a crow allowing a stranger to sit so near itself. They're too territorial.

She takes another drink of her bad coffee and looks at the door to the conference room. She considers hiding under the table. It would be funny, anyway, the police officers would think she was crazy. She decides not to go under the table.

The door to the conference room opens and a woman police officer comes in. Fenella keeps looking at the birds, she waits for the officer to greet her. She corrects the officer's pronunciation of her last name; the officer sits down opposite her. Fenella smiles benignly and folds her hands around her cup.

"You were difficult to get hold of," the officer tells Fenella, looking at her file folder. Fenella nods. She doesn't answer her phone. "Your number was found in the phone records of the victim in an open murder investigation. Your number called his. How were you acquainted with him and why did you call him?"

Fenella can't remember calling him, then she does. She gets cold. The officer shows Fenella a picture. Straight nose, dark eyes. "Does he look familiar?"

"I must have called a wrong number," Fenella says. She looks up, meets the officer's eyes unexpectedly. She shakes her head.

"All right," the officer says and reaches to pull the paper back, Fenella's fingers are full of heavy pressure upon it, pinning it in place, she lifts her hand, smiles. Fenella watches it slide away from her. They have her, if they want her. The officer clips the paper back into a folder and closes the folder.

FENELLA, TRYING TO KNIT TWO STRANDS OF BLACK MOHAIR TOGETHER, RUNS INTO A SNARE OR SEVERAL. SHE HASN'T BOTHERED WINDING THE YARN INTO tidy balls and the two feeds of it have snarled round each other in what seems an irreparable mass of knots. Leaning forward from her pillows she tugs at the yarn; for such a slender strand, it will not snap. It's the silk core of it, harder than bone. She pulls harder, it cuts into her finger joint and whitens the fingertip, and she stops pulling.

Sighing, she drops the knitting and sucks her finger, three-quarters of a sleeve done, connected to two thin black threads that cloud out in their angry coil and neaten again in their separate skeins. She picks up the knitting again and this time tries with long deliberate fingers to unpick the fine strands one from the other, untangling this one running under the other, this one wound eight times round that one, undoing a knot here, a knot there, feeding the mass of the sleeve between the two, and it all leads back to more dementia.

From the bedside table beside the cup of coffee and the glass of water, Fenella takes up her embroidery scissors and makes four snips, two at the beginning of the knot and two where the knotting peters out. Limp strands of black hang from the sleeve, the two skeins, weary of their fighting, and the tangle lies freed in between. It looks like a black brain. Fenella tries to throw it onto the floor but it floats back down onto the bed two inches from where it started.

She does not want to wind yarn into balls, it's too boring. She looks at the unwound skeins and the incomplete sleeve. She's tired of knitting; her coffee is cold. She takes a drink of water and then dunks the yarn tangle into the glass. Drawing it out sopping wet, she rolls it between her palms, experimenting to see if mohair will felt. It does. When she has a tidy little solid ball of black, shrunk neatly down from that infuriating gnarl, she looks at it happily, full of a good idea; her sweater will be prettier with felted black bobbles on it. She will make several dozen.

But after making two more, finding that it takes a generous amount of time to felt each one, her mind catches on another more playful idea, and she gets out of bed to do it. When she was little, she liked to play a game she called Buzzers, which was tying a string from object to object and making an impossible net obstacle course she would try to walk through without brushing against the string and getting imaginarily buzzed.

She ties the yarn end from one of the balls to the leg of her bed and wraps it around a drawer knob on her desk. Unrolling the yarn in her hands as she walks back and forth across her bedroom, she loops it around the foot of her bed, a dresser drawer, the closet doorknob, to the bedroom doorknob, and she crosses the hallway and works her way through the bathroom, coming out and crisscrossing her earlier string into the foyer. She works around lamps, bookshelves, making a web over the chairs, into the dining room where she joins the second ball of yarn and creates a looping cage drooping from the iron bows of the chandelier and down around the table like a ball gown skirt of old, into the kitchen, through all of her appliances, the coffee pot, the French press pot, the stovetop espresso maker; through the knobs on all the cabinetry, the latches on the window, through the refrigerator door and the freezer door, where she ties it off in a big floppy bow. Black lines run through the kitchen, the apartment consumed by the black haze.

How strange that this was going to be a sleeve, Fenella thinks, carefully stepping, horse-stepping, high-lifted feet, through the buzzers back to her bedroom. A sleeve!

WITH LEGAL COUNSEL BESIDE HER, FENELLA ANSWERS, POLITELY, A FEW MORE QUESTIONS FOR ANOTHER DETECTIVE. FLORA, HER LAWYER friend, is here because Fenella wants to get this right. There are no coffees, no windows, and no amusing crows this time. It is so annoying that she must sit here and answer their stupid questions when her head is full of careful answers to the correct questions which no one asks of her but herself. She is thorough, she has an answer to everything. But all they ask is where she was at such a time and who she knew at such and such a place. All ridiculous.

She tries to care. She did this thing for some reason. She should care. And once upon a time, she really had cared. It makes her sad that she's lost this care. Sad and wasted. It's like being at a party with people who are not really her friends and who aren't really interested in what she thinks. It's depressing. She doesn't like it. She feels totally used up. She has always hated talking about things she has done, and this is a thing she has done that she doesn't want to stick her hand up and claim as her own.

She crosses her ankles under the table and folds her hands in front of her. No, she will not claim it now. Her hands feel too heavy. She feels too heavy. Everything is weighty. Even though the discussion is all about her and what she has done, it has nothing to do with her. She is so separate from this thing she has done, she no longer identifies with it as hers, and since they don't know that it's her thing, they can't discuss it honestly. So how can she answer? How can she talk about it?

They are waiting. She looks at her counsel, Flora. Her counsel tells her to answer. "It was more ignorance than an outright lie," Fenella says. "I didn't recognize him."

"You didn't recognize him, but you went out with him," the detective says.

"So what?" Fenella says, "I met him and he gave me

his number and I called him and we went out once and nothing even happened."

"You didn't have sexual intercourse."

Fenella looks questioningly at Flora; Flora yawns. Fenella looks back at the detective and shrugs again. She wants to take a nap. She's over it, she's over him. Does it matter what she says? What can they do to her?

FENELLA SNIFFS THE SHEAF OF SOMEONE ELSE'S SUMMONS. IT DOESN'T SMELL VERY MUCH LIKE ANYTHING, SWEET OR OTHERWISE, NOT LIKE HER own books that have a certain smell of their own. It smells dull like mail. She sets it down on Flora's desk, straightening the edges so the rectangle of it is pure.

She's sitting in Flora's chair behind the desk and Flora is across from her in a large leather armchair, her feet up and crossed on the other side of the desk, watching Fenella. The leather armchair is a magnificent piece of work, big enough for two people and hinged on a very silent swivel.

Flora and Fenella went to the same school and are members of the same club. Flora's older than Fenella, but not by much. "Your paper should smell of something," Fenella tells her. "Spikenard. That's a good one. Old-fashioned. Queenly."

"Why's that, why should it smell like something?" Flora asks and swivels.

"It's the signature of your work," Fenella says. "When

a person gets a paper from you, they should immediately know that it's you it's from."

"They do," Flora says, swiveling back. "It has my signature on it."

"A literal one," Fenella says, "but not a subtle one."

"Does your paper smell?" Flora asks.

"I don't really send out that much paper," Fenella says. "My books smell of me. Not at first, but they start to after they've been with me for a while."

Flora says, "I'll keep it in mind."

Fenella smiles. It's good to be humored. Flora's good for that, among other things.

"Now for the charges of witchcraft," Flora says, "I don't understand how you're going to manage that. I think you're being really stupid."

"Am I allowed to be amusing to a jury, if it comes to that?" asks Fenella.

Flora stares at her. She says, "Calm down. No jury, no court. Don't play."

"Play," Fenella scoffs. She is not playing.

"This isn't play."

"I'm playing myself right now," Fenella says. "How am I doing?"

Flora, looking down, shrugs.

"Do you think you should come with me if they ask to talk to me again? They made it sound like they would. I like it when you come, it's professional."

Flora objects, "But I'm not even a criminal lawyer."

"No," Fenella says, "no, you're right." She muses,

tapping her fingers on the shiny desktop. "I'm sorry. I shouldn't have asked."

"You're a mental madwoman," Flora says. "This is unreal. I can't believe you dragged me into this."

"Don't worry about it."

"You don't seem to be taking it very seriously," Flora says.

"Well, my god, why should I?" says Fenella. She stands up.

Flora leans forward, supplicating. "But Fenella," she says, "there is only so much that I can control, on my end, with what I have to do with."

"But Flora, you don't have to control anything," Fenella counters. "I assure you there is nothing to control. Nothing for you to control besides these elaborate legalities," she amends. "I've got the strings, you know."

"Wait," Flora says, swiveling stealthily in her armchair as Fenella crosses the room, "what are you going to do?"

"Well," Fenella says, and sits back down again on the edge of the table. Visions of dark things fill the air like vultures and land as plain words.

A CROW PROVES A POINT SOMEWHERE OUTSIDE BUT FENELLA SLEEPS. SHE'S GOTTEN HER WISH, SHE HAS A DAUGHTER, SHE IS A MOTHER, IN A DREAM. This is a dream. She's a good mother. She knows she is. She herself has had such a good mother, there's no chance for her to be anything but.

Fenella and her daughter aren't writing stories at the kitchen table, and no large birds are coming. Fenella and her daughter are outside already, unafraid of any bird. They're right outside a building, standing in a little brick alcove. The brickiness is exaggerated in Fenella's dream. The walls of the building seem very thick and big. Fenella's wearing fantastic sunglasses that would be ridiculous in real life, but in her dream, they are perfectly proper. Her little daughter is indeed wearing a dress, but her little daughter is not quite proper-daughtery. There is something wrong about her as if she isn't really a person at all, something in her appearance which is a half shade off from perfection and gives Fenella an eerie feeling as she looks at her.

Her not-quite-right daughter shrieks and holds her arms up to Fenella. She stamps her foot. Her face is pink with screeching.

Fenella looks down at her daughter. This pink face! This tantrum! It's so familiar. This happens all the time. Fenella says, "I am certainly not going to pick you up if you shout at me."

Her little daughter screams and cries. People walk past them and stare and go inside the building. Fenella ignores them, smug; she has a daughter, her very own. What they think of her and the situation is irrelevant. This is the universe, right here, incubating in this open bawling mouth.

"Pick me up!" her little daughter screams.

Fenella kneels so she is face-to-face with the little creature. "Look now," she says and takes the little pink face between her hands to make her little daughter look at her. Her little daughter looks at her and screams, a terrible, ragged thing of a sound ringing from the edges of an ancient world. Fenella laughs; she has the power here. She feels like spring. Fresh and green and indestructible in her coming hence, all sweetness pouring out of her, unstoppable, changing the world. "I'll pick you up, only don't scream in my face," she says and picks up both of her little daughter's hands and holds them.

Her little daughter chokes and hiccups. Her screams taper off, she's calm. She holds on to Fenella's hands and looks at her with wet eyes.

"Poor little one," Fenella says. She breaks the connection to the little soft hands and puts her own hands onto the sidewalk and pushes herself up. Up, up. Now she's taller than she's ever been, it makes her dizzy. She shrinks back down a little and puts her hands into her pockets. She has pockets, big flat pockets. There's stuff in the pockets, candies, coins, keys. She draws her hand out of a pocket and looks at the array of things on her palm and picks out a hard candy in a waxed wrapper. "Here you go," Fenella says and gives it to her little daughter.

She looks up at the sun even though there's a roof there. The sun looks like a pearl.

Now her little daughter's really choking. Fenella kneels down again and shakes the little daughter's shoulders. The little daughter chokes harder. Fenella stands back up. "I don't know Heimlich," she remarks. Other people walking past stop and watch too.

"I don't know Heimlich," Fenella tells them, and they nod and walk on as the little daughter chokes and dies and Fenella observes.

Now Fenella wakes up, lies fascinated. In bed, she lies like in a coffin, on her back, hands folded at her belly, completely unnatural for her; normally she sleeps curled about a pillow on her side. Is it real? Could it be real? What would it be like, to dispose of a thing like that? A thing that is her very own. Her very own, very special thing. *There is so much in this world to try*, she thinks and closes her eyes again.

"I'D GO BACK AND REDO EVERYTHING," FENELLA SAYS DREAMILY. SHE WALKS ABOUT IN FLORA'S OFFICE LIKE AN ACTRESS IN A PLAY, MOVING FROM PROP TO PROP and occasionally thoughtfully touching them. Flora, in her comfortable leather throne, her legs crossed at the knees and her hands folded on her knees, swivels gently to and fro on the pressure from the ball of her foot touching the floor, following Fenella's movements with temperate consideration but a mismatched look of skepticism on her face. She's wearing an amazing pair of shoes; Fenella has the website written down in her black notebook so she can purchase a pair when she gets home. They're old-fashioned high-heeled oxfords like a witch or an English lady of the manor might wear, black suede with whirly pale embroidery on the vamp and heel. Beautiful! Quite beautiful.

Fenella drifts behind Flora's desk and looks from this vantage point at Flora's feet. Generally, it's low form to copy another lady's footwear, but since she and Flora don't share the same walk of life, Fenella thinks it's perfectly okay on this occasion to do so. They will never run into each other at a bar. Fenella doesn't go to bars anymore. They will never meet on the street because Flora drives into the city from the suburbs. Perfectly, perfectly honorable. In fact, Fenella could take them now, it would be a simple matter of shoving a pen into Flora's ear to get her down, then Fenella could run off cackling with the pretty shoes. But why deny herself the pleasure of waiting for a postal box, and all that? she thinks, and walks around the side of the desk, stroking it with her fingertip. "I had a friend in high school," she says.

"Just one?" Flora asks.

"Yes, just one," Fenella says, "and she was kind of a floaty sort of whimsical person, you know, always sort of seeing art in things."

"Yup," Flora says, "I know the type."

"It was annoying," Fenella says. She looks off into the distance and remembers. "I was perfectly happy to sort of let things seep into me, and you know, do their work from within, but she always wanted to express herself. Ugh. Anyway." She stops staring at the northwestern corner of the ceiling and switches to a place beyond Flora's left ear. "She said to me once, actually she wrote it, in a note, we were always putting notes into each other's lockers, she said I need to fall in love, and I quote, 'real love, my kind of love, not your kind of love.'"

"What was your kind of love?" Flora asks, "molestation of small animals or something?"

"Oh absolutely," Fenella agrees. "But the strange thing is, is I know what she meant, even though I don't know what she meant. You know? And now I think," she says, dreamily again, walking in a twizzling sort of way across the length of the room with her hands poised out at her sides, "I absolutely think, she was a very perspicuous, no that's wrong, perspicacious, that's it, a very perspicacious lady, to be able to tell at the young age of sixteen that my type of loving something was very different from her manner of doing so, especially, especially since I had never loved anything yet. Don't you think?"

"Very perspire-y indeed," Flora agrees.

"So," Fenella announces, putting her hands up in the air and then putting them on her hips, "that's what I was thinking when I was doing it. How she would be very disapproving of Fenella behaving thusly. And that was when I knew that I knew what she meant. Isn't it funny," she says, dropping into a chair, "what kinds of things cross your mind at any given time? It isn't surprising, because it's a brain, but really. It doesn't need to be such a smart aleck all the time. But she was right, that's what I mean. Right ho, she was right."

"Right that you should fall in love the right way?" Flora asks.

"Well, no," Fenella says, "I think more that she was right about the essence of the thing, and I was thinking about it again, and I started thinking, how easy it would have been to do things differently, how very easy, instead of doing what I did to him, but then, you know, I couldn't have done it. The whole world would have to be changed in order to make it go that way. I would have to be a different person to do anything differently from how I do it. So it wouldn't have been easy. It would have been unnatural. It would have been hard. Very, very hard."

"I think most people surmount their natural impulses on a daily basis in order to fit into society," Flora tells her.

"Do they?" Fenella asks. "How?"

There's a silence. Fenella waits.

"Wait, are you actually asking me 'how'?" Flora asks.

"Yes."

"They just do. It's natural."

"See, and this is natural for me," Fenella says, "so you see what I mean."

"Then what did you mean, you'd go back and redo everything?"

"That I'd go back and redo everything," Fenella says.

Isn't it making sense to Flora? She stares at Flora, trying to find out. Flora uncrosses her legs and puts both feet on the ground as if she is about to stand up and get away. Fenella tilts her head to the side and imagines her own anklebones in those shoes.

"Well, what became of this friend?" Flora asks. "You've never talked about her before."

"Oh, she died. When we were eighteen, she killed herself."

"I'm going to tell you something, Fenella," Flora says after a minute, "and I don't want you to take this the wrong way."

"Absolutely," Fenella says. "I pay you to tell me these kinds of things."

"I think," Flora says very seriously as if imparting dying advice to an heiress, Fenella listens attentively as suits such a discourse, "that you are a frightening and a dangerous person." Fenella averts her face at this like she once saw a wonderful actor do when a lady told him she loved him. She nods. She knows what she is. "I know what I am," she says.

WITH A SPRING IN HER STEP, FENELLA OPENS THE DOOR WITH HER HIP AND CARRIES THE BUTTERED ICES OUT THE FRONT DOOR AND PUTS THEM down on the little table where her sister Theta's sitting. They're at that place on Grand where buttered ices are the specialty drink. The sun is high and light in imitation of Fenella's soul. She wears the copies of Flora's shoes; she hopes Flora doesn't come strolling down the sidewalk or they will have to fistfight. The shoes came special delivery, specially fast. Such fun! "And then he kisses the head witch's hand," Fenella says, sitting down across from Theta, takes a sip of her drink, swallows, continues, "and that's why it's good to be a witch, good things happen like that. I'll buy a doorman for my apartment," Fenella decides.

"Or you could stay at a hotel," Theta offers.

"Oh, Monteleone," Fenella says. "Eating oysters and wearing witch shoes. How perfect."

"Witch shoes do not a witch make," Theta says and leans back in her chair, as decisive as one who has made a cutting and winning thrust.

"It was white and there were pink flowers on it going all the way up to the sky," Fenella remembers fondly. "But that's like saying, a cancerous tumor does not a cancer patient make."

"That's such a stupid comparison."

Fenella doesn't hear, Fenella is walking in her mind in her witch shoes out the front doors of Monteleone and looking up, up, up the creamy road to the sky splattered with pink flowers and then down down down at her dark vamps on the crooked southern sidewalk. She gets dizzy and smiles. "I was never a witch until I put on my first pair of specially made witch shoes," she says. "I remember it like it was yesterday. All of a sudden, the divinity tickled my toes and came up through my soles and ran through my spine like the shivers and blackened my brain and a special witch cape unfurled from my shoulders and there I was, the lady that sits before you, a witch in lady guise." She nods at Theta. "That's how it happens. Soul's honor."

"Why don't you go there?" Theta asks. "South again."

"I can't," Fenella answers.

"Why not?"

Why not? Fenella shrugs. "I don't know." She takes a sip and considers things. Maybe she could. It might help.

"It would be hot," Theta says.

"Why would I want to be hot? Are you trying to get rid of me? Why don't you come with me? Come with me, Theta."

"I can't, I'm pregnant."

"So? You can come even if you're pregnant. I don't mind."

A silence falls. They drink their drinks quietly. "You know," Fenella says, "I made this dream come true."

Theta puts her glass down and looks around. "Which dream is this?"

"This one," Fenella says. "This one, right now. I made it."

"This one what?"

"This very one you're in right now," Fenella affirms. "The other day when I was with Flora, she had these shoes. And I had a daydream, I was going to buy those shoes, and I was going to sit out in the sunlight with an icy drink and crossed legs and witch shoes, and look at these surroundings, and tell me I did not make this dream come true."

"That's not a dream come true," Theta says. "A dream come true is a goal you've worked for. Something."

"In a limited sense of the phrase, yes. But if a lady dissects the little words from the accepted meaning, my meaning is equally valid."

Theta snorts.

"I had a dream," Fenella announces, "and I made this day up." She looks around at the scene of her creation. Everything is perfect. Everything is just as it should be. Everything stinks of Fenella. "You maybe aren't even here," she tells Theta. "You may only be in my dream and having your own somewhere else."

"No, Fenella, I am actually here," Theta tells her.

"Possibly," Fenella says, still looking around, "possibly."

I THOUGHT WITCHES WEAR POINTY BLACK HATS," THE FAT MAN SAYS AFFABLY. FENELLA BLINKS UP AT HIM. THERE'S A YOUNG GIRL WITH HIM. ONE HAND IS ON her hip and she has a café au lait cup in the other. There's gum in her mouth that she moves noisily around. Fenella can hear it even over the banjos to her left and the bronze band to her right. Fenella makes a judgment on her and looks back at the man. He, more than the younger girl, is in the mood for indulgence, Fenella can tell. She has a way of knowing these things. Fenella straightens the sandwich board next to her. It says Witch on it, nothing else. She made it in her hotel room last night. Now she's sitting on a bench in Jackson Square in a black silk slip dress and her witch shoes, her skin glazed with light sweat and sunlight, sipping a whiskey and soda.

"I'm one of those modern witches you hear about," Fenella tells the man, touching her hat. It has no crown, just a leather brim. She likes to let the sun touch her head. It's a warm hand, fingers in her hair, it illuminates the dark brain. "This is Baptiste Viry."

"What like Wicca?" the girl says, shifting her gaze to Fenella.

"No," Fenella says. She points at the black undertaker's hat upturned on the ground next to her feet. "That's Lilly Dache," she says.

"Is she a witch?" the man asks.

"No," Fenella says. "She was a hatmaker."

"For witches?" the man asks.

"Yes, possibly," Fenella says. "Her hats often came with hatpins."

"Happens," the girl snorts breathily. "The hell is a happen?"

"A hatpin," Fenella explains politely, "is what a lady used to stick through the hat into her coiffure to secure the hat to her head in case of a sudden gust of wind."

"Wouldn't a witch be able to stop a gust of wind?" the girl scoffs. The man looks at Fenella expectantly.

"Malefic witches are all around," Fenella says

vaguely. "No one has her fingers in all the pies. Another interesting thing about hatpins," she says to change the subject, "take, for instance, this hat, this hat came with a hatpin. Now I'm unable to secure it to my coiffure, because as you can see I don't have a coiffure"—Her hair's loose about her shoulders, very witchlike.—"so I could use it, for example, to simply jam into the side of my head, sort of to self-lobotomize, and it will also affix the hat in place. Would you like to see?"

"You're going to jam a pin into your head?" the girl asks.

"No," Fenella says, "I was just joking." She smiles at them. "But pins have been used since ancient times in all sorts of witchcraft. In England, they still every now and then dig up old bottles full of pins and hair. They find them under thresholds and things."

"What kind of spell would that be for?" the man asks.

Fenella tilts her head and thinks about it. "For countermagic. Pins are otherwise useful, too, as a type of image magic," she says. "To make someone pay for their misdeeds. Or to call a witch to your presence so you can accuse her of being a witch. That type of thing. There's a very interesting story about Henry the Fifth when he was a prince. He was dismissed from Council and came to the king's presence in a robe full of needles to apologize."

"This Henry, he was a witch too?" the man asks.

"Now that," Fenella says, "is an interesting theory. His brother, his little brother, he had to do with witches, dreamy Humphrey. He once killed a poor French trumpeter for getting on his nerves. That was Henry. That is apropos of nothing, though." Fenella looks over at the brass band. They are being highly magnificent at the moment.

"Isn't that voodoo?" the girl asks. "Sticking pins into dolls and stuff."

"It can be."

"Are there a lot of witches down here?" the man asks.

"There might be," Fenella says. "I'm a northern witch."

"You just come down here for the heat?" the man laughs.

"No, I wanted a beignet," Fenella says charmingly.

"Ha ha ha," the man guffaws. He unfolds a billfold from his pocket and tosses a five-dollar bill into Fenella's black hat. Fenella smiles. She has made over fifty dollars sitting here and telling people silly facts about witchcraft. You can do things like this in New Orleans. Fenella asked, last night when she came in, the woman in the perfume shop where she bought her cake of lavender-scented wax. "Does one need a permit to put a hat out for alms down here?" and the woman replied sourly, looking out her open door at the opera singer bellowing across the street, "No." "And here you go," Fenella says, taking a pin out from where several are stuck in her wristband and pressing it into the man's palm. "Use it for your next witchcraft." The girl pulls at the fat man's arm, they walk toward the brass band. Fenella adjusts her hat and waits for the next.

"The devil has nothing to do with witchcraft," Fenella says irritably in the shadow of the cathedral. This morning, her audience is a young silly Gothic couple who want to talk to her about demons. The boy has two solid sleeves of tattoos and the girl's hair is missing any shine from the black dye coating it. Even the sun won't be lighting it up. They sit on either side of her on her bench, all of them watching a violinist send candied notes into the clammy air. "That's a Christian invention, and a Continental one, and a silly one."

Clouds are over the sun today and humidity swirls damply, coldly, through the square. Fenella's legs are all goose-bumped over. She's wearing a short fluffy skirt and a black sweater. The animal fibers of the sweater are caught with the stink of the old dark bar she was in last night, the smells, sweating out of the old brick walls, of caramel and cigar, sweat, and oldness. The fresh air will clean it out for her. Her hair needs a shampoo, though. A man who saw ghosts put his hand in it. A trumpeter called for heat, and Fenella kissed a hot dog seller in the street.

"I'm English and German by ancestry," Fenella tells the Gothic pair, "so the witch creed I inherited is mixed Continental and insular influence, and being a pure American girl, and an American witch, with freedom to do whatever I like without fear of persecution, mixed with what I know of English and German witchcraft, I wouldn't be worth my salt if I bought into the bullshit trope that true witches worship or ever did worship the devil. I mean, I suppose it is possible that certain persons, who happened to be witches, also did have some Christianity in them and therefore did simultaneously worship the devil. In that case, I would argue they were less witches than they were Christians, because witchcraft is the same thing as Christianity, a state of mind, and to have two conflicting states of mind is also a state of mind so, those poor people. Three states of mind. Can you imagine?"

"So, like," the Gothic girl says, "it's all a state of mind. That's cool. But I know this girl, we know this girl," "Alyssa," the boy says, "And she was possessed," the girl says, "by, we swear to god, a demon. She knew it, we all knew it. She was literally sick. Like, spewing. I mean it was full-on possession. And then she died."

"And you think a witch did it?" Fenella asks.

"No, it was a demon," the girl says. "I just said that."

"Yes, well," Fenella says, "in the old creed, witches sent the demons. That's why there was the connection, and the Inquisition. So who was the witch?"

"I don't think there was a witch," the boy says.

"Well then, like I said," Fenella says, "devils have nothing to do with witchcraft. You want to go talk to a Catholic or something because I don't know a thing about demons or possession or whatever it is you're talking about. I think you're pretty silly, actually."

"That's kind of a bitchy thing to say," the girl says, getting up.

"It's a witchy thing to say," Fenella says. She can't help it. When a lady stops appreciating a bad joke, she might as well die. She smirks. The boy gets up too and they both leave. They don't put any money at all into her Lilly Dache.

Fenella adjusts her Witch sign and settles back to watch the violinist. He is very, very good. The acoustics of humidity are wonderful. A sweet lick of wind runs over her legs. The sun, fixed behind a thin skin of silvery clouds, burns perfectly round and stilly, but heatless and colorless. Fenella crosses her legs to warm up, looks at the whorls on her shoes, and feels good. Part of the cosmos, she is.

It thunders. Southern thunder is different from northern thunder, there's a silvery sharpness to it, it cracks like hasty temper and is gone in a flash. Fenella lies in the hotel bed, listening to it. The bells of the cathedral ring through it.

Why am I here? she wonders. There is nothing to do. No one believes in witches anymore. Sorcery has gone out of the world. *One must be a witch in secret*, she thinks, *and not mind that no one knows or cares. But it's hard to be satisfied with oneself all the time*, she thinks, *and be the only one who knows it.* Sometimes a lady has an urge to prove herself, to show the world, this is what I am, this is why I am special. But definitely this is hard to do when what one is has passed out of the social belief of the world. Why is she here?

This is not good, this is not good at all. She must stop this. If she stops believing in herself for what she is, then what is left? Nothing at all. It is unbuilding from the inside out. Then the truth that everyone else sees will seep in, and the outer world will go dark and dull, all gloss lost, everything stupid. Why is she here?

This is her own fault, she decides, that she is trapped in this hotel room by bad weather, unable to ply her craft. Last night, she threw her rotting blouse brooch into the bathroom sink when there was still water in it from bathing her feet: that caused this storm, this storm is her making, and it is working on her unmaking. Witchcraft is a subtle art, full of tricks, and if she doesn't watch carefully, she will outplay herself.

She's swinging her legs over the side of the bed, she's going to walk through her storm to get a cup of coffee, flout it in its face as it were, when her phone vibrates. She answers it, it's Mummy. Mummy has bad news. "Theta's miscarried," Mummy announces.

"Oh, no," Fenella says and sits up straight on the edge of the bed, crossing her legs. She pulls her hair over her shoulder and begins to plait it, wedging the phone in place between her ear and shoulder, "Is she perfectly all right or is she very upset?"

"It was very early," Mummy says.

"Oh yes, yes," Fenella murmurs, "very common."

"Nina miscarried her first pregnancy, and I did too, I told her."

"Sort of a family tradition then," Fenella says. "Are you very upset?"

"Me?" Mummy asks. "Why would I be upset?"

"Well, I don't know," Fenella says, finishing her braid and drawing a hand up the length of her leg, "you love babies."

"She'll have another," Mummy says with complete assurance.

"I want a baby," Fenella says. Mummy laughs. Fenella retorts, "What does it say of the world, do you think, that witchcraft's proved false, and marriageless pregnancy is still full of immorality?"

"There is nothing immoral whatever about Theta."

"The words change to fit the tune."

"What?"

"Nothing."

"Was that thunder?"

Fenella stands up. "Yes."

"It's not even cloudy here," Mummy says.

Fenella pictures her looking out a window. "I'm in New Orleans." Fenella picks up her shoes from near the door and carries them over to the bed.

"Fenella! Why did you not tell us?"

"I don't know," Fenella says, sitting back down.

"Well, call your sister," Mummy says. "I don't think she's too upset but she still likes to hear from you."

"Okay, Mummy."

"I just wanted to let you know."

"Thank you, Mummy."

"Bring me back some of that coffee, if you think of it," Mummy adds.

"Okay, Mummy." Fenella sticks her feet into the black booties and bends over to lace them.

"Hope you're having fun," Mummy says. "Love you, honey."

"I love you too, Mummy," Fenella says. She stands up and wriggles her arches into place.

"Bye. When are you coming back?"

"Bye," Fenella says, not answering. She hangs up, sits back down, and folds her hands serenely in her lap. She smiles, she smiles. All healthy tissues restored to her, like a healed consumptive, this sweet balm of news. This is why she is here. She did this, this is hers, her gentle action, flung from her hot palm into the wild world. *It's good to be a witch's sister*, she thinks, and pushes nimbly off the bed. It's good to be a witch's sister.

SHE'S GOING HOME TODAY, SHE'S IN HER TRAVELING SUIT, AND SHE HAS HER LEATHER SHOPPING BAG OVER HER ARM. IT'S ALL SHE BROUGHT IN THE WAY of luggage, she didn't bring very much to New Orleans at all, she doesn't even really know how she managed to get here. Planning is not her forte. It amazes her that she's even managing to leave.

As she leaves the hotel, a lady recognizes her as

the witch from the square and accosts her outside the hotel gate. As she approaches Fenella, she does it just as if approaching a fawn, with her hand limply out, her expression one of approbatory favor, as if meeting an old English-speaking friend in line for the firing squad in an uncivilized country.

Fenella's hackles go up at her. She is small, she actually wears gloves. *Who wears gloves in summertime?* Fenella thinks, but it works as a hook on her own interest and she hangs back from the curb, the airport van will come when it comes, and concedes to answer the lady's question. *She must be a real witch too*, Fenella thinks, *she's checking me over*. So Fenella gives a frivolous answer to the question, How does she know she is a witch?

"I think it began when I was very little. When I was very small, you know, in age. Literacy, it was what did me in, really. Literacy. I mean, really, if anyone wants to look at where the world went wrong, it was when literacy became rote and necessary for everyone. Some powers, leave them in the hands of ones who can hold it, I think sometimes. Now everyone, and everyone, can, and all the worthy, pure, good conclusions get lost in the piles and piles and piles of meaningless words. I think a medieval world is sweeter. But anyway. I could read when I was four, I could read full novels in first grade. This is where it starts for me, books. All the books. One day, I was reading the Bible. About the Virgin Mary. I didn't know why they kept calling her 'Virgin

Mary' so I asked Mummy, 'What's a virgin?' and she told me to look it up in the dictionary." Here, Fenella gives the lady a meaning look. "And I did, and it said, you know, something like, 'one who hasn't had sexual intercourse.'" So I went back to Mummy and asked, 'What's sexual intercourse?' and she said, 'Sweetheart, go read something you understand, please.'" Fenella leans over to scratch her ankle. She stands back up. "And then because I could never then understand why it was so special that a woman had a baby, the import never struck me as anything spectacular, so I did, I read things I understood. All of my children's books about witches! And I understood those. You know, in the cold place in your soul, the mint of it, I mean, where you recognize what is what without any explanation. No one needed to explain to me what a witch was. You grow up knowing. I grew up knowing. That's how you can tell made-up concepts apart from real ones. If you have to ask for an explanation of something, it's not genuine. Even if I were illiterate, I would still know. Here comes my ride."

The white van trundles slowly down the narrow uneven street. The same man is driving it as drove her out from the airport. Fenella gets forty dollars out from her jacket pocket, and when the van pulls up next to the curbside, she leans in through the open passenger window and hands the bills to him. "I can open the door myself," she tells him. Then with her hand on the handle, she turns back to look at the other real witch. "You can't expect a real answer," Fenella tells her.

"Real things are always buried underneath the top things," says the other witch.

"Only in stories it works that neatly," Fenella says.

She swings the door open and gets inside. She looks once more at the other witch on the curb. What is her purpose? What had she wanted? Fenella considers her a moment longer and then slams the door shut on her. She hoists her leather bag onto her lap and folds her arms around it. Soft music plays, the van pulls away, the interior of it cool and dark and sweet as air conditioning ever is. The other witch made her hair prick up, her armpits prickle; Fenella's glad she got herself away.

In the library, Fenella meets another soul mate. Thinking vague thoughts about a variety of things while standing in line waiting to check out her books, they are all brushed away when the elevator from the third floor opens and out he steps, dressed all in black.

She puts her hand down when she sees it has fluttered up, up and slightly out, to claim something of her own.

He comes over and stands in the line beside her. She looks at him. Base inclination rails against common sense, she wants to put him in her pocket, she wants to take him home. He can live in her bedroom closet. She can take him out when she needs him. They can share clothes. They are the same, Fenella can tell. She casts a witch's spell to make him turn and see her.

He looks at her, she smiles. He smiles, he looks down, he looks back at her and smiles again. See, he recognizes her too.

Fenella goes on spinning the story. She brings him coffee cognac. She wears his sweatpants, she braids his hair. She pours cream in her coffee and watches him make toast. He fingers her sleeve between his fingers, they sit in silence beside. Their soul comes out from the dark place and sticks to everything they touch, like fingerprints. They are together, forever.

He moves up in line. His line is moving faster than hers. Fenella draws in her breath, she is going to be left behind. How dare he. The cruelty. It's awful. *To show me this*, she thinks, *just a glimpse, for nothing. Just to show me he exists.*

There is nothing I can do now, she thinks firmly, even though she feels so frantic and anxious as he puts his books on the counter that she lifts to her tiptoes, *there is nothing I can do right now*. She trembles. She needs to finish what she's started, not start something new. She hates the world. She needs to concentrate. She's in the middle of something. *Not now, not now*, she begs the world. *Not now*.

She stares hard at him. Not now, not now. He looks right at her staring at him as he walks away from the desk. There is a feeling of being slapped awake. It all goes cold. No, not now. She should be relieved but she's not. He walks past her, he shows her his back.

She watches helplessly. He half turns and smiles, uncertain, toward her. Fenella won't smile back. This world, this despised world. She hates it. She hates it well and fully and totally, utterly. She's glad she will die someday. Better to die than live in this taunting world, that draws a treat out of her pocket, half out of her pocket, showing Fenella what she has when she knows Fenella is forbidden from taking.

Fenella moves up in line. She looks over her shoulder. He is going down the stairs, he is going down the stairs, he is going, he is gone. Fenella, still here, looks at the empty space, she can feel it, the swirling, total emptiness: she hates it, she wishes she were dead. She has seen and she can't forget.

"You can't just get rid of it," Flora says, leaning forward, frowning.

"But I need to make room," Fenella answers. But she isn't being truthful. She got rid of the head long ago. She's just playing with Flora. What better to do?

Flora stands up behind her wide desk. Fenella, across the room, stands with her back to the door, gazing out the windows behind Flora. "Oh my god, for what?" Flora says. "Fenella, they aren't looking for it and they aren't looking for you right now anymore anyway."

Fenella knows this. She twists, as if upset, the top Medusa button on her black plaid jacket. Her miniskirt matches, she is wearing high shoes, not the pair she and Flora share. "I'll drop you as a client," Flora threatens.

"No, you won't," Fenella says, "remember, remember, the fifth of November, and all that, et cetera." She puts her hand down at her side. It is so difficult to stand with one's hands still at one's side! They would always like to be fiddling and folding.

"All of that aside," Flora says, businesslady-like, brushing aside all thoughts. Fenella smiles, remembering them, making Flora remember too. "All that aside, Fenella, remember where this started, why, why, why, are you turning it into this other thing now? This fantasy. Before it was simple. It was you, insulted."

"I was not insulted," Fenella says.

"You were fucking absolutely insulted," Flora insists, "and it was that, it was only that, you were humiliated, and now you have gone off the goddamn deep end with this utter fantasy."

Fenella curls her lip a little bit. She touches the branch of lavender pinned to her jacket. She presses a leaf between her fingers for a distraction; a sudden violent smattering of rain blurs the windows. She brings her fingers to her face and breathes in the chilly scent; the rain ceases. "I wasn't insulted," she tells her palm sadly. Flora has misinterpreted everything, everything. Fenella kisses her own palm, pretending she is someone else doing it. "It wasn't about that at all. I wanted to see what it felt like."

"You were, you were!" Flora shouts angrily. "You were humiliated because he fucked you and dumped you, and you were just like every other goddamn girl in the world, and there was nothing you could do about it, so you did this, this base thing, and you brought me into it, because you are a selfish, horrible, frightening, perverse bitch."

The play is over now, it is all over. Fenella knows, this is truth, she cannot turn it back to play. She does not like this view of herself. It splits her into twins, making her feel odd and slippery, this sudden, simple notion that she is like others, but she isn't: she lifts her head, others have not risen above as she has. Others have accepted, and others have accepted a defeat. *I tore a hole in the world*, Fenella thinks, *I took my teeth to it, I started the world over again for myself. It is no fantasy, what I have become. This is as real as myself.*

The pin slips out of the fabric and the lavender floats to the ground, a little wilted. Fenella picks it up. The rain starts up again, dashing into the glass with such a noise Flora whirls around to look into the suddenly gray, slithery world. She turns back and stares at Fenella. Fenella shrugs. "Well, I guess I'll go then," she says, "now I know what you think about it, I just wanted your opinion," and stands there.

Flora turns back and stares out the window. "It's pouring out," she says wonderingly.

"It'll stop," says Fenella. She goes out. Down the long elevator and hallways, the real Fenella walking a springy slight step ahead of her. At the glass doors letting people out, she stares outside. Everything is becoming completely drenched. She pushes both doors open and goes out the middle of them. Protected by the flapping black awning, Fenella drops her brooch sprig and grinds it under her shoe, muddling it to a leafy paste on the sidewalk. A gust of misty rain dusts her bare ankles and knees like sugar. It hails for a moment, clattering down angrily upon metallic car roofs, and then, like an indrawn breath stuck in the throat of the world, it all stops. A woman across the street lowers her umbrella, shakes it out, and looks up at the sun. Fenella observes dispassionately. She doesn't feel pleased, she doesn't feel amused. She's tired, she wants to sleep. She sets off toward home. What better is there to do?

THE TRUCK IN FRONT OF FENELLA ON THE HIGHWAY IS THE EIGHTEEN-WHEEL KIND HAULING A BIG SHINY CYLINDRICAL THING. *USED TO MOVE GASOLINE, or something like*, she thinks. She's driven behind them before. Who hasn't?

She steps off the gas a little bit and falls farther behind the truck, and takes a ladylike drink of her coffee with her pinkie finger sticking out. She drove far out of her way to get coffee this morning. It's cloudy, cold, she didn't want to walk for it. She didn't want to stay in either. One of those mornings when everything is twitching and the brain in a fervor to move, move, move. She must have had a whip-up of a dream. One froths at the bit and doesn't remember why, because something happened, that didn't happen, yet happened.

It's a nice morning for a drive, the sky pearly, the highways smooth, and the driving is soothing. As a baby, Fenella used to be driven around in the car by her mummy and daddy to stop her crying and make her go to sleep. *I must have liked it*, she thinks. It still works good as a charm. She's soothed.

She takes another drink of her coffee. She wrinkles her nose, it's too bitter, there's not enough cream in it. When she gets home, she'll put more in. The saving grace of home.

Pressing the gas, she moves forward a little faster. The posterior of the cylinder has two inset red lights, and a bar probably used to open some secret hatch. It's dull to look at. She glances in the side mirror. A white car's coming up behind her in the left lane. Fenella hates white cars, she has a mania about them. She stays in her right lane and eases off the gas again. She keeps creeping closer up on the eighteen-wheeler without noticing. The white car passes alongside and Fenella takes another look in her mirror, but now there's a whole line of cars coming up. Following the eighteen-wheeler is hypnotizing her. She blinks to reset her eyes, then looks at the pale sky above the cylinder. It stays so still compared to the seventy miles per hour down here, she can't even tell she's moving.

The sky is more interesting. Above and ahead, an enormous flock of black birds float, slowly drifting together in a large whirly organized cyclone. They catch the wind in synchrony and turn their bellies toward Fenella, pale bellies. They fade into the smutty sky. They turn back and are black again.

Fenella's lips part and she holds on to the steering wheel with both hands, leaning forward to see them better out the front window. Black to pale, they turn, pale to black. Oh, it's a dream. It's lovely. She slows down to sixty so she won't pass under and lose sight of them as fast. The eighteen-wheeler gains considerable ground on her and the white car shifts into the lane behind it. Fenella doesn't mind. The superstition says white cars in front of her are better than white cars behind.

The chorus of ballerinas in the sky pivot to black, dip to pale. Lavender branches whipping in the wind. Her grandfather once said, when the silver sides of leaves show, it's going to storm. She wonders if the same logic applies to bird swarms. She drives under them and they drop out of view completely. If she hires a hack surgeon, they can cut out the part of her brain that says You Are Fenella. Then she can move in time with the world without trying to surmount it and be like the birds. *Oh, dreamy dreams*, she thinks. She drops her head back against the headrest. It's so disappointing to be a person, you can never be anything else. The world is a prison for persons and everything.

She fiddles with the gas pedal and pulls up close behind the white car. White cars! Only sociopaths can drive white cars. It's a proven fact. She ticks on her turn signal and moves into the left lane, jamming her foot down onto the gas and zipping forward in a delightful gust. She passes the white car and makes a wicked face at the driver inside as she does. She passes the eighteen-wheeler. As she moves back into the right lane, the bird flock comes back into view, this time shaped into a wavery V, making a hasty flight toward the west like Fenella. *The end, it cometh*, she thinks, and follows them speedily.

"Oh, hold on just a moment," Fenella says and looks into her handbag. The handbag is too big and black, she can't see anything in there. She sticks her hand into the depths and feels around. She finds her little black notebook and pulls it out, then opens it up and flips through the cards in its back pocket. "Here," she says and hands him her membership card. He looks at the front and back and gives it back to her. Fenella tucks it back into the pocket and drops the notebook back down into the leather pit. He opens the door for her and she sweeps inside grandly. Her handbag strap catches on the doorknob and pulls her backward. Kindly, he unhooks it for her as if he is letting a dog off its leash. "Thank you," she says.

She hasn't been able to relax. Her thoughts are high, lifting her up by the ears practically, making her almost float, and are accoutered in sharp edges. She wanders down the hallway and peeks into the rooms with open doors. She doesn't feel like opening closed doors. She goes into the bar and waits. She hooks the black suede-covered heels of her shoes around the back rung of the barstool. Her bag flops limply beside her feet. She looks around the bar. One woman says to another, "It's all about keeping the dignity of the position," and the other nods sadly.

Then with a gust of sweet air and black coat, Flora is sitting beside Fenella. Today, they wear the same shoes. Fenella turns her head slightly toward Flora. What will come will come. *The gods creep on with feet of wool*, she thinks. Sage Kit Marlowe. She licks her fingers, they are still buttery from breakfast.

"Well," Fenella says then, at the same time Flora says, "Well," and Fenella says, "Well, what then, please?"

"Well, I've done it," Flora says.

"Done what?"

"I've removed you from my client list."

Fenella shrugs. "Well, whatever, witches don't get lawyers anyways," she says. "Can I get some coffee and cream, please?" she says to the bartender who has begun to hover.

"I want to see your witchcraft now," Flora says

maliciously. "It's only what I've done that's kept them off."

"Think what you like," Fenella says, "you're only doing everything I've hoped for."

Flora snorts.

"You know I want to be executed for witchcraft."

"They're not going to execute you for witchcraft, you moron," Flora says. "They're going to put you in jail for being a psychopathic murderer."

"No," Fenella says, "they won't."

"Just because it's still on the books doesn't mean they ever prosecute anyone. Besides, no one who actually confesses to witchcraft has ever been executed."

Fenella shrugs. "I've already begun planning my defense," she tells Flora. "You should hear all the weird things I've found out."

The bartender brings the coffee and cream. Fenella lifts the cup and takes a dainty sip, flicking a dot of liquid from her finger, it smatters Flora's knee, Flora looks down and sees the shoes are the same. She becomes furious. "That's why I needed the month," Fenella says, "to do my research."

Flora makes a sudden gesture and Fenella, out of instinct, jerks quickly backward. A graceful arch of Fenella's coffee sloshes over Flora's feet. The pale handpicked embroidery turns mocha, the suede is completely wrecked. Fenella bursts out laughing.

"That," she says, "is your fault. Completely your

fault!" She points at the sad shoes and laughs. She feels slightly hysterical.

"Fucked and dumped," Flora hisses. "That's you, everywhere, and all the time. Fucked and dumped!"

"Who even cares?" Fenella says, stopping laughing. "What other people do doesn't matter to me."

"I hope they break your ankles," Flora says. "I hope they torture you and break all your bones and cut out your tongue and put pins in your eyes."

This reminds Fenella of something, an old image-fragment of something. "Did you ever happen to see Guy Fawkes's signatures from before, and then from after he was tortured?"

Flora stands in the puddle, proudly pushing her shoulders back. "No," she says, "but I hope I get to see yours."

"Well, tra-la-la," Fenella answers.

At the bar, trying to divine the message swirling in the golden spiral of cream she's just poured into her coffee, Fenella sees something very strange. In the flex of her left hand, there's a glint of metal. Something thin under the skin with the bare edge pricking out. It's a needle.

Bemused, Fenella touches it. There's a little ridge over it, barely perceptible, of skin. She tries to roll the thing around and make more of the exposed bit come out. It's like a sliver but instead, it's a sewing needle.

Tilting her head down over her palm, she gets her fingernails around the tiny shiny bit and tries to tug it out, but her fingers slip up around it without making it budge upward at all. She wipes her sweaty fingers on her napkin and tries again. This time, holding on with determination, it comes up and out of her skin.

She holds it between her thumb and forefinger, up to the pink light over the bar, and wonders how it got in her hand in the first place. It hadn't hurt coming out. It was like the game they played in elementary school when all the small girls would thread pins through the tip-top layer of skin at their fingertips and wave their hands at one another, pretending to be witches or bats. The teachers confiscated the pins and sent letters home. This now is what that felt like, sort of a dainty pull, nothing harsher. There is no blood.

She turns her hand palm up again, looks very closely, and sees another needle sunk in there. This one's a little bit deeper. She pushes up at the base of it, nudging it upward, until enough is poking out of her skin that she can get a steady pinch on it. This one she pulls out too, again, it comes out without injury, smooth as pulling a fork out of cream cheese.

She puts the needle down next to the other one and holds her hand up to the light. It's full of needles. They show like very thin dark seams against an otherwise transparent cloth. She grits her teeth and sets to getting all of them out. The bartender, passing by on his way to rinse a glass, makes a strange face.

Fenella doesn't know where the needles came from at all, she doesn't remember putting them in her hand. For each one she pulls out, another seems to show up, as if they are packed in there in layers, like fish on ice. She creates a little pile of needles next to her coffee cup in getting them all out.

It doesn't seem, she tells herself as she adds another to the bunch, *as if that many needles would fit into a human lady's hand.* Of course, maybe they came to be in her hand quite naturally, maybe she, without knowing, put her hand down in a place full of needles; maybe in digging around in a drawer, they came to be in her hand. Well, she doesn't remember it, but that doesn't mean anything. Once, she heard a story of a girl who swallowed a pin and didn't know it until her lung deflated. This could be a similar case.

When her hand looks clear, she flexes it and holds it back up to the light. All of the dark little seams have disappeared. She runs her thumb over her palm. The skin is smooth. When they played the pin game as little girls, there were always little perforations at the fingertips where the pins had punched through, little tunnels under the skin, and sometimes the skin would tear and the tunnel collapse.

Maybe, she thinks, *it's because this time there's only an entry point.* The needles never came out the other side. This might make a difference. She takes a drink of coffee and wonders why she hadn't noticed the needles before now. It seems they should have been making it very difficult for her to use her hand at all. *Oh well*, she thinks.

"Have you ever encountered a lady with so many needles in her hand?" she asks the bartender. He frowns as if he doesn't know what she's talking about, even though he does. Fenella plays along and shows him her needles. "Maybe I'm not even a lady after all," she adds and laughs. The bartender wipes the glass and doesn't even smile, he doesn't care what she is or isn't. Fenella laughs at that too.

Outside, everything is crystal, everything is pure. The air is a black crystal, sooty on the outer edges, but full of clarity, full of nothing. It is the miracle of seeing made apparent. Then it gathers itself and breaks and the darkness pours in. All sound has quite stopped, except for a full rushing in the ears.

This storm isn't one of Fenella's storms. She peers out from underneath the shop awning, clutching the coffee cup folded in her hands like prayer. Her hair drips at the ends. She tilts her toes up in her sodden flats disappointedly; she remembers a childhood book in which the weather wrecks the heroine's suede shoes. Remembering this makes her happy, Fenella smiles, she is a heroine too, in someone else's story for the moment, she thinks. *Whose storm is this anyway?* she wonders.

Suddenly, all personal thought is stripped away: the

wind wracks up and writhes around her, shudderingly, tightly, then flaps on past. Openmouthed, she watches it go. A garbage can balances upon its back wheels for a bare moment and tips over; a branch smashes into a car door. Then it spreads like a claw and plucks up a table, an umbrella, throws them furiously into the street center. A car swerves. Fenella smiles again: ghastly!

Another wave hits her. She's startled backward, her coffee jets out of the little mouth opening in the cup lid and is caught by the wind, flayed to a million pieces, and spreads across Fenella's face like a foam. Surprised, she spits and blinks and drops the cup and puts her hands up to the wind. It pushes them back into her chest and her against the building front. She's held there. She can feel where the brick gives way to glass right at her thighs, it's quite painful. She waits. Her hair undone whips across her face, her clothes sponge-like, cold and massy, press to her skin. She laughs, thinking they are all that hold her body together in this terrible strain, but her mouth is stuffed with wind and the laughter makes no sound.

She watches as the street before her is ravaged. A car goes to its side. A pair of pants floats quite ethereally on by. Her coffee cup, by some strange chance caught in a tiny off-spiral of the greater blow, tumbles around and around at her feet. She tries to kick at it and free it from its frantic circling, but she can't move, not a limb of her will move. *It's come for me*, she thinks. She doesn't know what she thinks it is but here it is, she thinks, here it is. As if waiting for her to know, and now knowing that she does, it assents, it lessens its pressure, Fenella released from its bond stumbles forward. Now she can move in it. The vortices create a little path, just for her, for her alone, she is special.

She's pushed out from under the awning. Something smacks her ankles, it's the coffee cup, freed as well, it rattles happily down the street away from her and mixes with all the other garbage flowing westward. Fenella tries to turn around and get back under her awning but can't. She looks up curiously at the sky. She stretches her hand up. She touches the sky. When the cloudiness hangs so low, what else is there to say she is doing? *This is a dream*, she thinks. This is unnatural.

She crouches down to get away from it and wraps her arms around her knees. The wind boxes at her ears. *No*, Fenella tells it, *I'm not coming yet*. It presses down around her with another great effort of suction but she refuses. It lets her know its displeasure, furiously battering at her back. *No*, Fenella tells it, *no, no, no*. She feels sorry for it, it is trying to do her a mercy. It flings trash at her. *I don't care*, Fenella thinks defiantly. Then acting as if it never cared about her at all, it wanes to a flutter; it swirls over her back and is gone. Fenella waits. Slowly, sound presses down to its normal place. A sickish, lunar light replaces the thick darkness.

Hearing her own breathing, Fenella stands up. She puts a hand up wonderingly. The ceiling has lifted. She looks at the refuse around her feet, no longer flowing, inert, as if it never had any motion at all. Fenella touches her face in awe, she is still here, so is the world, she can't believe it, the laughter pours out. Somewhere far off a man is yelling, "Holy shit! Holy shit!"

THETA," FENELLA SAYS HYSTERICALLY, "THETA, THETA, DID YOU SEE HIS FACE? DID YOU SEE HIS FACE? OH MY GOD, I CAN'T, I CAN'T," SHE HAS TO stop walking because her laughter has overcome her. She leans over and leans back practically choking with it. Theta's small hand lands on Fenella's back and the sound of her laughter snakes through the air around Fenella's head. Her face comes into view beside Fenella's. Fenella is leaning over with her hands on her knees like a runner now. She looks over at Theta. They both start laughing again. They clutch at each other and begin walking again down the sidewalk. There are still gobbles of garbage in the gutters from yesterday's storm.

Fenella, with her arm about her sister's, sobers, she sobers with merriment, with too much laughter, a steadfast soberness of complete immersion in a moment that is happening now, it leaves no room for anything other than its own swelling feeling.

Her sister is much the same as her. Their waists are the same. Fenella stands a bit taller. Theta's edges are softer. She is a delicate version of Fenella's sharp dark side, the softened shadow of a cut-glass angle. Beside her, Fenella feels rough and grating. She feels complemented. She feels completed: her arm about her sister's similar waist, the heavy dark strands of her own hair pasting to her lipstick, whipping out through the wind, tying themselves in slippery knots with Theta's frothy curls, and in her own turn, by the vicissitudes of the wind, its own special contrary prerogative, getting a mouthful of that stuff sprouting in such natural pretty disarray from her sister's head. She spits it out. The wind gives her a taste of Theta. She licks her fingertip and, putting her hand down by her side, offers it to the wind in thanks. *I'm so happy you're not pregnant*, she thinks. *I'm so happy that's all over with.*

She tightens her grip on Theta's waist and digs her fingers into the skin. Theta squeals and Fenella snorts and they have to stop and take another laughing break. Theta pinches Fenella's upper arm in revenge and Fenella shrieks. Passersby smile as they get a whiff of the high delight. It sweeps out, this type of merriment. It spreads until it has spread far too much and there's nothing left at the center of it, the center brooms it all back, everything vanishes into it. *I am the center*, Fenella thinks, *I am the source*. She is high, supergod-like in this moment. The moment travels on, she goes with it, it is too too perfect to let go on alone, they are two priestesses walking hand in hand down an endless aisle. Theta says something.

"What," Fenella says, "what did you say, cherished one, I was not listening," and she tilts her head and looks at her sister's mouth moving but fails again to hear the words coming out, *it doesn't matter*, she thinks, *it doesn't matter at all*, and she smiles, and she laughs again, seeing their reflection in a storefront window, "Oh, look at us Theta, we look like the gorgons."

"It's been so windy lately," Theta complains and brushes a curl out of her face. "Oh," she says, coming to life and squirming out of Fenella's arm as they pass a cafe, "I want some tea."

Fenella nods. "Run in and get a cup. But I'm not coming in, I want to stay out in this clear air."

"Don't you want any?"

"No. Okay, maybe a sip. I'll have a sip of yours."

All good things get sucked inside the store with Theta. Fenella stands waning on the sidewalk, waiting with her arms wrapped about herself. Now she's nothing. She hugs herself tighter. Her hair blows all around her face. She can never do this again, the vacuum is too severe. Her sister, her sister. *I won't call it back*, Fenella decides suddenly. *I'll let it go: I can go with it.*

Theta comes back happily with her steaming cup. Fenella gratefully takes a sip and slips her arm back around Theta. She loves Theta so much, she decides to make an offer. "Next time you have a baby," she whispers to the sponge of hair, "I'll protect it with my spells for you."

Theta shrugs Fenella away, "Oh no," she says, "you keep your spells away from my baby."

They walk separately now. Fenella casts secret sidelong glances at her sister as they go. *It doesn't matter*,

Fenella thinks again, *it doesn't matter what Theta thinks. She is familiar to me. She is the most familiar: it doesn't matter what she thinks.* But it does. She looks straight ahead now. For now, it's best to walk alone.

"She's two weeks," the other woman says, and Fenella overhears, "two weeks old tomorrow."

Fenella pushes her armful of books across the desk and looks over. The other woman is loose-skinned and soft, wobbly with a post-birth body. Fenella, who has always been ectomorphic, is fascinated by pregnancy and the way the body mutates to accommodate such a thing. *What does such a strange change feel like?* she wonders. If she had allowed Theta to remain pregnant, she could have asked her. What is it like to change so much for another person's benefit? And what sort of person would one even have to be to consider allowing such a change?

A different sort of person than myself, Fenella thinks. She could never allow it. But she looks at the baby and feels left out. The baby head sticking out from the woman's arm is hung at a strange angle, the eyes are closed.

Fenella gets her library card out of her purse and hands it to the worker, still looking over. The baby is perfect with swirls of dark hair growing up from its scalp like black meringue. "That hair," the worker at the other station comments.

"There's a fine on your card," the worker helping Fenella tells her.

"I know that," Fenella says. She wishes he wouldn't interrupt. The sleeping baby hangs there perfectly swaddled in its mother's arm. The closed eyelids are thin crescent slices in the spotless flesh, the lips, lovely. A flat pig nose, like all babies have. Fenella looks at the mother. The mother's nose is not so bad.

"You have to pay some of it today," the worker says to Fenella.

Fenella looks back at him. "Oh, fine," she says, she digs deep into her bag, fishing for money, she keeps looking back over at the other station. She finds a dollar bill. "Is a dollar enough?"

"What?" asks the worker, he's been looking to see what she's looking at.

"A dollar." Fenella holds it out. "Is a dollar enough to pay?"

"Oh. Yes. Let me get you a receipt." He turns to ring it in.

Fenella, freed for the moment, sneaks another look at the baby. *What other world is this?* she thinks.

Coming back to her with the receipt, the worker starts to check out Fenella's things. Fenella crumples the slip of paper he's given her in her fist and watches him now. He handles the books carefully and slowly.

I was a baby once, Fenella remembers, bored, and looks back over at the other baby. *What if the baby were dead*, she thinks, *and the mother is just carrying it around because she has gone insane?* She smiles. People do all sorts of strange things. But the baby opens its mouth and baas. It is alive. A band of crooning erupts from its attendants, the infatuated mother and the admiring worker. Fenella's own worker stops his scrupulous stacking by size of Fenella's books and looks over and smiles too.

The mother puts a finger on the baby's cheek. The baby immediately stops making the awful goat noise. Fenella is fascinated. She whips up a quick spell and causes the mother to need to scratch her own face. The baby, severed from its mothertouch, bleats and bleats. The mother, in an imperious gesture, rubs a thumb over the tiny forehead, twines a lock of baby hair around her forefinger. The small mouth closes.

Fenella looks back at her books. The worker pushes them over to her in a perfect pyramid. "Thanks," she says.

"They are due back in three weeks," he tells her.

"Yes, I know that." She wraps her arms around the books and pulls them off the counter. She brushes past the mother and the baby. She stops and turns around as if moved in a secret compulsion, and says, laughingly, because the words come up of bilious force and not by her own choice, "She has amazing hair," and laughs again. What business does she have talking of a baby? She shifts the books in her arms. "I had hair like that when I was a baby too," she says for an excuse, and by way of letting them know she too was once a human.

"Oh, and look at it now," the mother says.

"Gorgeous," the worker helping the mother chimes in.

"I would just love her to have hair like yours when she grows up," the mother tells Fenella. "It's beautiful."

Fenella, abashed, looks at the ground. "Well, thank you," she says, "thank you." She looks up and meets the mother's eyes, smiles foolishly, and quickly walks away, embarrassed.

SHE FISHES THROUGH THE AIR AND HOOKS FLORA'S ELBOW. FLORA RECOILS FROM THE SNATCH BUT FENELLA HAS HER IN A GOOD TIGHT GRASP. SHE pulls Flora back from the direction Flora's feet were making, little black arrow steps, winding with small clicks to the east. Now the compass has stopped and turned to face Fenella. Around them swim corporate logos and pale tired faces above dark suits. The city buildings rise gray and hollow, the sun not yet high enough to illuminate the streets. A bronze forerunner of it slices through an adequate gap and brandishes a blinding spark against a tinted window, the window's wreathed in metallic flame. They tilt their faces away from it.

"What do you want?" Flora says, the sound of the want loud and terrible, and shakes her elbow, trying to get rid of Fenella. Fenella pulls her closer in. They are nose to nose and eye to eye. "What are you doing?" Flora says, wriggling, "I have an appointment." She flings her arms up and down and kicks at Fenella, trying to get loose. People turn to look. Fenella holds on. Flora stamps her feet in rage. "You insane woman," Flora says.

"Just stand still for a moment," Fenella says soothingly.

"For you, nothing," Flora says and doubles her attempt to repel Fenella. She kicks Fenella's shin finally and Fenella loses her grip. Flora spins off and Fenella is after her immediately, she grabs her collar, pulls her back in. "Let me go," Flora chokes and kicks, but kicking backward is a hard thing to do. Fenella puts her hand on Flora's neck and walks around to the front of her. She pats the collar down and shows Flora her palms.

"Just stand still for a moment," she says again.

"Witch," Flora hisses. "Dog-bitch."

"I got rid of it a long time ago," Fenella says, "I just wanted you to know."

"I don't give one little finger for what you've done," Flora says, "or when."

"I understand your hateful disposition," Fenella tells her. "Let me get your shoes fixed for you."

Flora laughs, a shrill, hysterical cackle that cracks through the loitering bus engines. "As if," she says, putting her face closer to Fenella's than Fenella had come to hers, "I would put anything I possessed into your furious fingers. So it could come back to me like poison. Like a whip. As if I would ever do something so goddamn fucking stupid!"

"I know a suede specialist. She could fix them. Oh, just let me do it. I feel bad."

"Oh, liar," Flora says. "You laughed. You laugh about everything."

"What else is there to do?" Fenella says. She's said this before. "If you're going to be so superstitious, I can just write down the name for you. You don't have to give them to me. You can take them yourself. I won't put my hands on them. I won't touch anything of yours."

"They were mine first," Flora says sullenly.

"They are completely different objects," Fenella says. "Mine, and yours. I'm sorry I got coffee on yours. I'm sorry I laughed."

"Are you sincere?" Flora asks. "Are you sincerely sincere?" Now she gets Fenella by the wrists and draws her near. The mascara blacking her lashes together into long threads, the darker freckle near her pupil. Fenella looks at them with tenderness.

"I'm sincere," she says to them. "I would never do anything to hurt you."

"Liar," Flora says, digging in with her fingernails, "you want to kill me. I know what you did. I know what you are. You'll kill me. I know you."

"I'll protect you," Fenella breathes out. "I'll keep you here with me. You know what I did. You know what I am. You are the only proof I have of what I am. I would never do anything to hurt you. Just let me give you the name of the suede specialist, she'll fix your shoes. I shouldn't have laughed."

Flora releases Fenella. She regards her. Fenella nods. She reaches into her black leather bag, the deep one, she's been carrying it all week, and gropes about for her notebook. "Do you have a pen?" she asks, searching with her fingers the bottom of the bag and feeling nothing. "Do you have a pen?" Fenella asks. "Snap out of it, please, a pen, please." She looks up. Flora has her little concealed-and-carried handgun out and pointed up under her own chin.

"Tormenter," she tells Fenella, meeting her eyes, "witch, sociopath," and in this spin of words, she pulls the trigger, thc sunlight shatters over the buildings, Flora falls in her puddle of blood at Fenella's feet.

And she sits looking at the shoes. She kneels in front of them. She smirks. They could never be cleaned, not by an expert, not by any soul soother. Flora let them stew too long. The suede's nothing more than a gummy brownish crust now, all softness gone, just cheap, old, dirty. The whirly embroidery is full of filth, like little tornados that have picked up a whole countryside they will never drop. She sighs. What will she even do with them? *Another thing to get rid of*, she thinks. But she keeps looking at them. There is something wonderful in them. Something of her own hand in them. Something in them that she set afoot. She smirks again. She cannot keep her good wit down. Her wit is a spleen exploding its waste. From the bowels, from the mouth. Like a head exploding its brains, see there again, she cannot stop it, her wit. It's set in perpetual motion.

The moon will keep spinning, she thinks, *the earth will keep moving*. With such ballast for examples, what should a lady do but the same with her wit? *What can a lady do but the exact same?* she thinks. There is no stop to anything.

She has given Flora a gift. Murder is a gift humans give to other humans so they don't have to wait to die, so they don't have to do it to themselves. Murder is a pair of sturdy leather boots over the rutted bad road to death. It is a dark and warm furred coat, to ease into the winter of death. *We would all just have to kill ourselves or wait for death*, Fenella thinks. It is a cold, long wait. Flora wanted out.

Except she doesn't really believe this, she is just playing again. Or is she? It makes sense to her. She touches the hard shell of the shoe's toe with her fingertip. The nubby embroidery she strokes, like she saw the mother stroke the lovely baby's forehead. She kisses the slipper's toecap. She licks it. What a taste! Here's old coffee and the sourness of warm cream. Hints of asphalt, and underneath it all, the scum of calfskin, the bare flank of a stripped animal under her rough tongue, for a minute, she's kneeling with her face stuck in a bloody animal's side.

There will be a funeral for Flora. Fenella will attend. Flora was a prominent woman, yes, prominent indeed, very businesslike in the walk of life. Fenella laughs aloud. The walk of life, she slays herself with this superfitted humor, her good foot-themed wit.

Maybe a comedienne, she thinks, *maybe for something new to do*. No. She is what she is. It is determined. The roots of a lavender will never spring an oak. Whatever other goals she had, gone, gone, gone, flayed away into this new Fenella. This usher-of-death Fenella.

I am happy with this, she decides. *I have never felt so utterly like myself.* It is a lovely thing. She laughs again. How great it is to recognize one's self.

Fenella stands up. She uncurls her legs and stretches, she lifts her arms over her head and stretches, she stretches her neck, everything, to its limit. She yawns. She looks around. *Back to the old problem*, she thinks. She goes and fetches the box for her pair of the shoes out of the closet. Her pair can stay out, she wears them all the time. They live by the bedside and the front door and on her feet.

She picks up Flora's shoes one by one and stuffs the toes with crumpled and thick gray paper, she ties tidy bows in the short suede laces. She double-knots and adjusts the tongues. She fits them into the box, neatly lying atop the cotton shoe bags, and lids the box. The full box goes into the closet. This is something no one will come looking for. This is a safe trophy. *Something to show the grandchildren*, Fenella thinks, and laughs, and shuts the closet door.

I*S IT A COUSIN?* SHE WONDERS. SHE MADE THAT UP IN HER OWN HEAD. NO, HE SAID IT. OR DID HE? SHE CAN'T REMEMBER. IT DOESN'T MATTER. "NO, I WAS a client," she says to him. "I did know her before however. I'm very sorry."

"Well, I hope she didn't leave you in the lurch or anything," he says and laughs. "You know. Not off to jail or anything. Left without your advisor. And whatnot."

Fenella wrinkles her nose a little bit. "No, not at all," she says politely. "Nothing like that at all. She managed my money affairs, is all."

"Oh, one of those," he agrees.

"One of what?" Fenella inquires.

"Oh, one of those, you know, unexciting ones," he says.

"I think she mostly did unexciting things like this," Fenella offers. "It was her specialty. She was very good."

"Oh, yeah, yeah," he says. "I wouldn't know, not one of these, you know, cake-eater types." He looks down at Fenella's shoes. "So what do you do, money stuff too?"

"No, I don't work anymore." To keep his confidence, she adds, "I used to."

"Good for you," he says. "What'd you do, money stuff?"

"No," Fenella says, "I worked at the library."

"Oh yeah, right on, right on, a librarian!" he says enthusiastically.

"Well, no, technically I was not a librarian," Fenella admits. "I shelved books."

"I love the library," he goes on. "You can get anything there."

"Yes," Fenella agrees, "yes, you can."

"Yeah, you look like a librarian type." He looks her over. He moves his hand up and down. "Very straight up and down. You know." Fenella nods. "So'd you get fired or quit or what?" he asks. "Bet they've got good benefits. City job, right? Government package. Nice."

"Yes, they were very nice benefits."

"And union too, I bet," he says.

"Oh, yes."

"Job security," he says.

"Yes," says Fenella.

"I could go to the library every day," he confides in her. "That big one right downtown. They've got everything. Computers too."

"They really do," Fenella agrees, "yes, yes, they do."

"They've even got *Playboy*," he says and laughs. "You can just sit right there and look at *Playboy*. I mean, come on! Who knew! At a library. You can just sit at a table and look at *Playboy*. Can't on the computers, though. They got that stuff blocked."

"Well, they have to," Fenella says. "But you can ask them to unblock it for you."

"Well, yeah, yeah you can," he says sadly. "But then they treat you like a dirtbag. You know. They come up and walk behind you all sly-like. To see what you're looking at. Seems like that's breaking some privacy law or something, I would think. To spy on what someone is doing on their computer. It's cheaper than going to the clubs anyways. Yeah, much cheaper." He sighs. "But they're all so, you know," he makes a wavy gesture in the air, "not like," he moves his hand up and down again. He looks at Fenella. "I like the tall lanky type."

"Mm," Fenella says, "yes, I would bet there is much more variety online." She smiles toward a place behind his shoulder.

"You could do that," he says encouragingly, "if you're looking for a job, you know, they'd put you up there. Sort of to break up the monotony and whatnot. Be a nice break from all the huge tits, I'd think. Lanky-like. Yeah."

"I'm very flattered you think so."

"Don't suppose you need the money," he says, "but for fun."

"Well, I will definitely consider it," Fenella tells him. "Thank you." She looks over his head. There are two men staring at her, their hands folded in front of their crotches, blocking the doors. She knows who they are. "I'm sorry," she says, looking back at the possible cousin, "I need to use the ladies' room before the service."

"Oh, nice meeting you, nice meeting you," he says. He puts out his hand to shake or to touch her but she ignores it. "It was a pleasure."

Fenella walks carefully away, keeping her face to the ground. "I'm sorry, where's the ladies', do you know?" she asks, touching a woman's arm, a woman who looks like she knows things, and follows the directions given.

In the stall, she sits on the closed toilet and crosses her legs, looking at her feet, clad in Flora's dirty shoes, and then stares at the back of the door, waiting, willing. The bathroom door opens and the shoes of men appear under the stall door. Fenella stands.

Spread your arms," they say, Fenella obeys. They're looking for the witch spot. A crowd of them, four, a fifth one coming in and going out to pass on information and bring back messages, and a woman in the corner by the table, carefully keeping her eyes to the ground, but Fenella sees her looking every now and then. Fenella rolls her arms in a tiny circle. It's tedious, and hard, keeping them straight out and still.

"Don't move," one of them orders. Another is at her right hand, spreading her fingers apart, examining closely between the knuckles. He finishes. Fenella makes a fist and rubs her thumb over her fingers, he grasps her left hand and pulls the fingers apart. His breath falls on her skin, hot puddles quickly cooled. At the same time he says, "Got something here," the man circling around her legs on his knees says, "Look, right here, I think," and the two standing off approach Fenella, the woman in the corner looks up.

"On her finger, right here," the one says, "pretty faint," and for a few still moments, Fenella's hand is a hot spot. They shine a flashlight on her finger, one rubs it to make sure the freckle doesn't come off. The door opens. "Get the photographer," one commands, and the door closes again.

"And here, this one," all the men get onto their knees, one holds on to her knee for support, another her calf, they are not young men, not goat-nimble anymore. *I am their scaffold*, Fenella thinks proudly. They run their hands over her pale leg, pulling the skin taut with their fingers, making the freckle there stand out with prominence.

The door opens. Over the men's heads, Fenella smiles at the messenger. He bobs his head and goes out again. The photographer comes in bashfully carrying a glittering dark heavy camera and doesn't greet Fenella with her eyes. Fenella is nude, and the photographer will not look at her, it embarrasses her to see Fenella, Fenella thinks, or it shames her. The photographer wears glasses and has thick hair and looks steadfastly at her camera instead of the body.

The carpet of men at Fenella's ankles rises up around her. "We've got one on her left finger, three-fourths of an inch from the knuckle," one instructs the photographer, "and another possible, two inches thereabouts above her left knee socket." They all move back as one dim mass into massier shadows, leaving Fenella at center.

The photographer stands off, holds the camera to her face and looks through it at the ground or Fenella's foot, takes it away from her eye and adjusts something, brings it back to her eye, and steps forward toward Fenella's left hand. She places the lens a hairsbreadth from Fenella's skin.

"I need a light," she tells the ground, "can you, like, shine that flashlight?" The one with the flashlight comes up and holds it over Fenella's hand. The photographer looks through her camera again. "No, no, not like that, more to the side, the left, and, like, down a little, okay. Hold it steady, please." As she talks, her jaw moves the camera. It touches Fenella's skin, it's cold, her hand twitches. "Sorry, sorry," the photographer mumbles. Fenella moves her face very slightly and watches the top of the photographer's head, the camera clicks echo through the cell.

The photographer steps backward. A man steps forward to point out the freckle he's found above her knee. Fenella can't watch what's going on behind her. She looks straight ahead, practicing perfection, and listening. Sounds are awesome when there is nothing else. Again she feels the cold circle of lens metal press against her skin.

"Do you need light?" the flashlight man offers, stepping up and going behind Fenella.

"No, no," the photographer says. The flashlight man comes back to the sideline of Fenella's vision, his head tilted, watching.

The chilly outline of circle draws back, and the mechanical, full clicks jaw through the space again. Then Fenella feels very light, very cool, the photographer's finger on her ankle giving a fast caress, she gives Fenella her honor. Fenella makes a face. There is no point in doing what she does. Fenella does not need it, this honor, from someone who cannot even look at her naked body without a glass in between.

The photographer says, "It'll be about fifteen minutes," and then Fenella hears her get up and sees her come around. She doesn't look back at Fenella as she leaves. She holds her camera carefully in both hands. The door opens and closes for her.

The man with the flashlight clicks it off. The sound of it is weak and unimpressive after all the heavy instrumental camera clicks. The men all look at each other and at Fenella. She stands still with her arms still out. One of the men opens the door and the three others stream out like a dark cloud converging into another. The last follows suit and closes the door behind himself.

The woman in the corner comes forward then. She puts Fenella's arms down for her and murmurs sweetly, "They'll be back once they've developed the images and examined them," and hands Fenella a glass of water. "Would you like a blanket?"

"No," Fenella says. She rolls her shoulders. "How long does that take?" she asks.

"I don't know," the woman murmurs again, "we've never done this before."

Fenella takes a drink of water. The woman doesn't

look at her but says, vehemently, to the floor, "This is wrong. This is wrong."

"Don't feel badly," Fenella says. "If something happens, it's the right thing to happen. If it were wrong, it wouldn't happen." She lifts her foot and rolls out her ankle muscles.

They confer in the corner again, and all leave again but one. Today they move her, she must go see the court. She sits quietly waiting, they are letting her sit today. They have been letting her sit a lot, they don't know what they are doing. The one left over comes and stands behind her with his arms crossed, his legs spread apart. Fenella can see him reflected in the tinted window of the door. He is all business. Fenella listens to him breathe and watches his reflection watch her head. The rest of the men come back. Fenella sits up straighter.

"Here," one says, separating himself from the others and coming to her, "you need to put this on." He puts it down on the table in front of her.

"What is it?" she asks.

"Vest," he says.

"Vest?" Fenella says.

"If you're going to be executed," he says, "it will be by the court and not some loony on the sidewalk."

"Ah," says Fenella. She laughs, she can't help it.

"Help her get it on," he says to the guard standing

behind Fenella. He gives Fenella a dirty look, they all leave again.

"I know how to put a vest onto myself," Fenella tells the guard. He shrugs. Fenella stands up and picks the vest up from the table. It's heavier than she expected. "It's so heavy," she says, laughing and holding it up to her chest. "I never thought they were so heavy." It's dark and slim and fashionable but full of secretive weight. She slips it over her head. It comes down like gravity. She is bolstered. The Velcro straps flap down her sides. She straps herself in. Her black smock bulges out the sides. They've given her back the clothes she came in wearing to put on today. "Am I wearing it correctly?" she asks the man. He nods. "Why wouldn't they just aim for my head?" she asks, very tritely; she knows this is a trite question but asks it anyway. "That's where I would be aiming, if I were aiming at a person."

"Most people aren't that good of a shot," he tells her.

"Oh," Fenella says, "I suppose not." She sits back down. "Could you shoot someone in the head?" she asks him conversationally. He snorts. "A criminal, I mean, of course," Fenella corrects herself. "I wouldn't dream you would do it for fun, of course."

"I've had the same specialized training as everyone," he admits grudgingly.

"I suppose it's a skill worth having in your line of employment," Fenella says encouragingly.

"Not of much practical use," he confesses.

Fenella laughs her special human laugh. He warms

up. "I'm a witch," Fenella says, "I can usually protect myself."

"I don't believe in witches," he tells her.

Fenella frowns, she doesn't like this, people must believe in things. "Then you're not much use to me," she says, "or them."

He shrugs. "I didn't ask for this."

"Why don't you believe in witches?" she asks, curious. He shrugs. "Disbelief is a fad," she tells him. All the old beliefs will come back eventually. She will see to it they will.

He snorts again. "Do you know what year this is?" he asks. "No way."

"Then what do you think I am?" she asks.

"Delusional," he tells her. Of Flora's school. The doors open and the men all come back in. Her guardian goes back on guard.

"On your feet," one of the men says. Fenella stands back up. They open the door for her. She goes out. One man sweeps around her to lead the way, the others follow her in train. They proceed down the hallway. They get to the front of the station and the leader turns around and faces Fenella. Fenella stops walking, obligingly, and waits for him to tell her what he is going to say. She is slightly taller than him. She corrects her posture so she is even higher. She smiles down on him.

"Don't speak to anyone," he says. "Don't look anyone in the face. Keep your head down. Follow my feet. We are in front of and behind you. When the car door opens, get in, shift yourself all the way to the other side, the side farther from the curb, do not lift your face from the floor, keep your eyes on the floor, do not peer out the window."

Fenella nods. She cannot imagine what he is talking about. He looks past her shoulders. Fenella pats down the straps of her vest. She likes the weight of it very much, it is easy to dream, in it, of absolute conquest.

"Cover her backside," the leader barks. "Someone get on her right side." He makes sure they are all posted in a form of perfection, then nods to the person keeping the doors; the doors swing open. The troop of men and Fenella march out. She looks all around her, keeping her head down, but she sees, she sees everything, a massive crowd of faces and lenses, and she can hear them too, watching the boots of the man leading her through the pale stream of sidewalk cleared for her, just for her, the toes of her favorite black flats following his boots, she hears the furor around her, rising like a river in flood, she feels a cold glow, she is proud, and hollow, and pure, a tube of fluorescence, this is for her, this is all for her, her accomplishment: and now they all play along with her. She climbs into the car. The door slams, the sound is proofed out. "God," she comments.

"Go," the leader says to the man behind the wheel. They go.

The judge sits at her high table. The prosecutors and detectives sit slightly below her, Fenella behind them, at her very own table, lording it from behind. She listens with interest. The only court experience she has so far had in her life is when she went in and lied to get out of paying a traffic ticket. It was easy to lie then and be believed. Now she tells the truth, she is gowned in truth, and they meet it mockingly.

"We have followed every protocol," one says to the judge. "Every single little protocol."

"And this protocol is coming from?" the judge says. She lifts her hands and looks around as if to find the protocol standing somewhere in the courtroom.

"This is not our decision," the same one says. "We have no choice. She confessed to it, and we follow the steps of the legal process now."

"She confessed to it," the judge says. "And 'it' is what? Please be quite explicit."

"She came in," he explains, "on our request, to discuss a suicide at which she was present, and to which she confessed, she did."

The judge looks at her papers. "And explain to me, please," she says to them, "how a suicide can be committed by another person."

"Homicide by witchcraft," the man almost shouts in his embarrassment.

"Homicide by witchcraft," the judge repeats.

"She confessed to it," he says again. He grows surer of

himself. "And, following the old charters, a confession, or someone who confesses, must be brought in and charged. We have no choice; this is the law."

"I am aware of what the law is," the judge says. "What I am not understanding is why you are following through on this so thoroughly. Surely you know we do not follow through on these cases anymore. These women go to doctors. Not through the court system. This is an embarrassment to the entire country. To the whole world."

Another man stands up. "This is my call," he says. "This is my decision. She will be charged with witchcraft."

"Your call," the judge starts to say, indignant, but he holds his delicate finger up to her and says, "It is my call, so says the protocol."

"Then why are you even here?" the judge says.

They at the lower table look at each other. "It's protocol," another one offers. He looks down and reads from a paper. "'The witch is brought before the judge.'" He looks up again.

"This evidence is laughable," the judge says. "Jurors will hear the word 'witchcraft' and laugh. Homicide by witchcraft. I'm laughing already."

"They will not laugh," one says. "This is a dangerous creature. She's confessed to causing one death. Howsoever she did it. I believe she did. We've discovered she's tenuously connected to two other vicious homicides, and we will connect her firmly to them now. She's a menace; she is a poison."

"You seem to have caught her delusion," the judge comments.

"Dangerous creatures need to be put out of this world," the one says, "with whatever means are given to us to do it. Madam, she's handed this to us. I will press on. And do not think I have caught her delusion. I am using the tools she is giving me, to make sure, and to do whatever I can do to make absolutely sure, she is stopped. That is all. Madam."

"Get out, all of you," the judge says. "I would like to speak with her. The witch." She makes a scornful noise. The men huddle and confer over the protocol. Apparently it says nothing to the negative, her order is allowed. They funnel out again. The judge comes down from her high table and sits across from Fenella at hers. They study each other. Fenella has never been this close to a judge, she feels a little giddy and excited. *How does one become a woman judge*, she wonders, *in this day and age*?

"I don't believe you are a witch," the judge tells Fenella. "I'm curious about you. Don't you have a mother? Father? Sisters too. Money, clearly. A nice family? Why are you doing this? Look at your shoes. You obviously have interests. You're extremely educated. I don't believe you have a sickness. You might be a simple murderess? I don't know. I can't even tell you what I think a witch is, in this day and age. I'll tell you what I think you are then," the judge says. "I think if you are a murderess, you are also a very arrogant and intelligent young woman. I think you might know law very well. I think you're hoping for this loophole to work in your favor. You might know you stand a chance of being charged with murder, and you know full well these witch laws are a joke. A joke! You know a jury will laugh, decide you are a sick young lady, throw this back at us, and you will walk free and never be charged with anything. Or, you are a very sick young lady, the rest ad infinitum, with the same result." She becomes quite angry. "I will never, never, allow a woman to be tried as a witch in my courtroom. This is the modern world. I will not allow this to happen. I cannot believe this is even happening. How dare you have the presumption?"

The empty, swirling space, the dark woods: they are not just for Fenella. She watches with fascination as the judge's foundations crumble completely, it shows in her face. *There is nothing like a human face*, Fenella thinks, *words are nothing next to it*. The trajectory of disbelief will blow away civilizations, and the only proof will be in their faces, and their faces will rot, and all will come back to the purity of nothing.

SISTERS! THE HISTORY OF THE WORLD KNOWS WHAT POWER THERE IS IN SISTERS. THE FATES, THE GRACES. FENELLA KNOWS THEM. THE MUSES, THE furies. His sisters have come to view her. She knows who they are. She has seen their pictures in the newspaper.

Fenella is open for viewing today, the last of the old

protocols, the last cracked fissure of protocol cracking wider, and pouring into it will come the shining modern world. Things will boil, things will change. The steam that comes up will come up to a different air.

She stands behind her pane of glass and watches as people come goggling past in museum lines and small clusters and look at her thickly, through dumb eyes and clever eyes. There is a kind chair in the corner if she gets tired of standing. She can only use it for five minutes at a time. Her mouth is gagged, she cannot speak, only think, but there is never any harm in that, only thinking. She is in her black smock and bulletproof vest and black flats, and she stands there silently.

And here are his sisters! She knows it. She can tell. She knows their faces. The heads of his family are all quite alike. They come quite near the window. Fenella stands politely open to them. *This is a dream come true*, she thinks. *I will make the most of it. I will make them remember me.* One sister wears a high pink silk collar, the other, heavy boots.

They study her and she studies them. Fenella wonders if they believe in her. She would like to tell them it is because of him, all because of him, that she is what she is. That she has become what she has become. She owes him a great debt. She owes them, they are his sisters. She cracked through him and came out herself, better. It would have been nicer to do it by herself, she thinks, but the world, like everything else, makes a lady go through an ordeal and follow steps to get the result she wants.

They stare at Fenella. Pink collar and heavy boots. They are just as she daydreamed them to be. Floating and mournful. Slightly accusatory, she had not imagined that. She supposes it's to be expected. Nonetheless, she is pleased to have this opportunity of meeting them. The gathering moves and they move with it. Fenella smashes her hand against the glass to stop them from going.

On the other side of the glass pane, they stop and turn back and look at her again. More people come forward to get a better look at what is occurring. The sisters are still and staring right at Fenella again. Good. Fenella, with a wildness, flings her body against the glass. She doesn't care what they think of her, what they know of her, but she owes them something: she gives them a spectacle; it is all she can give them from in here. Spit drips from the corners of her mouth. It is something they will remember at least. They will say, "Remember when we went to see the witch who killed our brother, remember when she threw a fit," and she will become a family legend, told over Thanksgiving, she will live in the family, she will be a sister of sorts. She flaps her arms. Whirling dervish, battering ram. She stamps her feet and throws her hair around. She laughs through her mouth gag, she is acting so silly.

The guards come in. One catches her around the

waist. Fenella kicks and kicks. "What are you doing?" he says, "Calm down. Calm down."

The people outside watch in awe. Fenella jerks her head back and catches his jaw with her skull, he lets her loose. "Oh my god," he says, holding his face, "oh, oh." Fenella shakes her head and slaps him across the cheek. The other guard pinches her elbows behind her back and twists her to face away from the window. "Don't lose your shit now," he says into her ear, "don't, you hear me, you have four more hours of this."

Fenella nods at the shadowy back of the cell, she nods, he spins her back around, the crowd is moving again, intersecting circles, forming curves, leaving. The sisters are gone. But Fenella's satisfied. She turns and smiles at the guards through her wet gag. She looks back to the window. The guards leave the little room. Now Fenella is alone again, herself.

A new crowd swarms in. Then Theta comes. Fenella walks as near to the window as she can, breathing on it. *Sisters*, Fenella thinks, holding out her hands, *my sisters*, and then she stops because only Theta is there. Theta's the good sister. Theta always comes through for her.

The door opens and a guard steps half in. "Are you going to do that again?" he asks. She shakes her head, it is her sister this time, she doesn't need to make a scene, she is already in the family memories. He goes out.

Fenella puts her palms up to the glass. Theta places her hands against them. The crowd around Theta works in a vortex, they thin out around her, they give her the space Fenella pushes them to give to her.

Theta looks around at the unmoving crowd and looks back at Fenella and says something. Fenella shrugs. Theta makes a communiqué of some sort, Fenella watches Theta's mouth move. Fenella puts her hand around an imaginary phone and pretends to talk. They will speak when this is finished, Fenella tries to communicate, she will call and tell Theta all about it then.

Theta begins to cry. Fenella taps on the glass to get her attention and make her stop crying. Theta's face is hidden by her cloud of hair. A woman comes up and puts her arm around Theta's shoulders; she looks like the other witch, the southern small witch with dainty hands. Fenella hits the glass angrily, violent-handed. The other witch look-alike looks at Fenella contemptuously.

The guards come back in as Theta is pulled out of Fenella's sight by the other witch. Fenella glares at the guards. "Behave yourself," they tell her. Fenella looks out through the window. Everyone is still poised in her strange suspension. She lets them go. They begin moving again. *What is the point of having sisters if they aren't happy for me?* she thinks. *Good riddance.*

The other witch, up beside the judge, stares serenely down on Fenella. She is lying about Fenella, spreading lies about Fenella, great big lies. She is saying Fenella is not a witch.

The other witch wears a cracked white dress. Fenella is still wearing her black smock. It has been cleaned for her. One of the lady guards has braided Fenella's hair with black velvet ribbon.

Fenella has amassed quite a court of ladies. She could have a coven now, any coven in the world could be hers, if it weren't for this terrible passion for disbelief. Everyone doesn't believe in witchcraft so strongly that everything of Fenella is conceived in the negative, she is not, she is not, she is not.

They forget she is a murderess, they forget she is wicked. All of that is smoothed completely out of existence by the absurdity of her claim to be a witch. So she is a scapegoat instead. She is a test of the system, the system will break around her, they say. They turn her quite, quite mythical! What they don't believe is in their right hands, they lick from the left.

This other witch knows, though, she knows Fenella is a witch and she lies ecstatically and hugely for some cross purpose of her own. The other witch's light voice of sugar spins over the silent court. Fenella listens interestedly.

The other witch tells them she herself is the leading legal expert in the western world in esoteric law. She tells them, Fenella came looking for her in New Orleans.

She tells them of Fenella's formal high education. She quotes bits of Fenella's research papers for their benefit. She informs them Fenella has led them all by the noses into her trap. She tells them Fenella is writing a book. Fenella had wanted merely to see how far an old law could be pulled. She desired empirical evidence. The other witch apologizes for her encouragement and assistance in the matter. She tells them, she thinks Fenella has taken things too far. She feels responsible. She fears for Fenella's sanity. Witches do not exist.

She stands up in her pale dress. Two guards hurry forward to help her down from the stand. She is a creature to whom people flock to offer their assistance. She comes around the side aisle, her shoes are slanting and black. She walks past Fenella, Fenella hears her stiff dress crackling against her thighs, and then she disappears out the courtroom door without even looking at Fenella. Like a wisp of cloud, gone.

The psychiatrist mounts the stand. He reads portions of the transcript of his interview with Fenella for the benefit of the jury. "Self: Tell me about your interest in witches. Accused: I don't really have an interest. Self: I don't think that's an honest answer. Is it? Accused: Aren't you interested in witches? Self: I'm interested in you and what you think about it. Accused: That's very nice of you to say so." He folds the page back and goes forward two pages. "Self: When did you first realize you were a witch? Accused: When I put on my witch shoes. Accused laughs. Self: I don't think you're being sincere. Accused: No, I suppose I'm not. I'm sorry, I'm not being very helpful. Self: Let's take another tack. Do you feel being a witch has anything to do with your identity as female? Accused: Accused laughs again here. Self: Why do you find that question so funny? Accused: Because it's so stupid. Self: Most historical witches are women. Accused: Plenty of men have been tried as witches. This is a patriarchy, no one cares about them. Self: So you see it as a good thing that witchcraft is a woman-dominated sport. Accused: I like that you call it a sport. It's sort of an individual sport. Can't you imagine the uniforms?" He turns over two more pages.

A famous feminist stands up and does her bit. The feminists have summoned a march for her, they come out of the woodwork and crawl over the world in support of Fenella. Masses of them. Some old-fashioned witches join in and young girls too, even like-minded men. Even Republicans are against this law. The world demands her immediate release and fights for the complete repeal of the witch laws. It has turned much more political than Fenella had ever imagined. She is highly amused by the whole thing.

If they knew, Fenella thinks wisely, *they would not fight for me. They would let it be.* But the murmur of masses is such that it softens the ugly face of honesty. It turns it flat and kills the details. It turns Fenella into a flat paper concept and strips her of everything true and personal. She is not a three-dimensional lady, she is a Victorian witch picture, made of crepe, thrown around like crepe, hung on walls, gentrified. She doesn't mind. It's a party, thrown for her, celebrated for her, or what a creation of her is in the minds of no one she has ever met. She is quite, quite universal!

The court goes into a recess and Fenella goes back to her cell in her black lusterless smock.

FENELLA SHINES TODAY, TODAY IS HER DAY, TODAY SHE IS BETTER THAN THE SUN: THEY CAN KEEP A STEADY FIXED GAZE ON HER. SHE DOES NOT encourage them to turn away from her as does the flustering sun with its flurry of brightness fending off all eyes like a dance of hands battering away onlookers. She is a dark sun today, a medieval eclipse today, today eyes cannot be torn away from her, not if she did the tearing out with her own two hands. This is fun. She is a fascinating person, they have deemed her this; *it is nice to be validated*, she thinks. She closes her mind and opens her mouth and lets the words blow out in whichever direction they wish.

The studio is white and bright, snaked with black cords, black cameras, all sorts of blocky solid black apparatus, she wants to keep looking at it, there is so much of it to look at. Her eyes move over it all as she talks, speaking ladylike, sitting ladylike, her hands folded in her lap, her ankles crossed in her own whirly shoes, her words go one way and her eyes rove another. She wears the same dark suit she wore for her first polite police interview, the makeup man has accentuated her eyebrows, her hair is pushed back from her forehead in a puff and trickles limply over her back and right shoulder. Men move about behind the wiry apparatus, wires coming from their shoulders, furious snakes bearing Fenella's sounds, she loves it, the drama of it, the great work to bring her silly words elsewhere.

The interviewer begins. "So, you confessed to being a witch."

"Yes, I did," Fenella answers, "I voluntarily confessed. Yes, I voluntarily confessed that I was a witch, it had to do with a close friend's suicide occurring right in front of me, she died, you know, right in front of me, and it was an enormous shock, it took a toll. I said, I did it. We had a history, we had played witch together. I just blurted it out. We had helped each other out through tough times. I felt at fault and said I had done it. This was how it started, and after that, the great machine of American law took over. I was aware this was still possible, of course, but I never thought it could go on like this."

A cameraman and a man with a clipboard are having an intense reading-over of something, Fenella wonders what it is they read about, someone drops something, and a rubbery echo dislocates through the sound stage, she meets the eyes of her cameraman and smiles at him, he looks away from her.

"Well, no, I am not very politic, though, yes, the Supreme Court carries its own aura of impressiveness, one cannot get away from that, when something crawls that high, it is very impressive." She chances to look upward, the ceiling, it is amazing, all black, squared with places for lights, places where panels have been removed and lights stick through, though the best ceiling she has seen so far was in a theater where she once saw Shakespeare played, the delicate attention paid to a theater ceiling goes beyond all measure of this one, nice as it is.

"Well, it was fascinating, I mean, and I suppose I am of a nature that goes where fascination takes me, and doesn't fight it, because really it was a very interesting experience, and if somehow I ended up being hanged for being a witch, then, well, that was a life, my life, and how it's ended up, it's written out, history has written it out, that is my life, that was my life." She zones back in, the center of this lady's face is the lock, Fenella fits her key into it, the fuzzy focus goes sharp, the interviewer asks, "Do you think it could happen again?"

"I think it would take a particularly special set of circumstances," Fenella says, concentrating now, "like the ones that were mine, how they all came together, forming this outcome, there are a million ways to get to a certain point, but it needs a convergence for it to be the same." She smiles, that which she has just spoken was gibberish.

"And do you think," the interviewer asks, "if mistrial hadn't been called, you would have been called to account for the murders that you are supposed to be responsible for?"

"Murders, no," Fenella says. "I love life." And she smiles.

"Can I ask how you kept your spirits up while this was debated in Washington?" the interviewer says. "You were held, were you not, in isolation the entire time. Did you love life then?"

"I was allowed books from the library," Fenella says, "and my sisters visited, really, it was not terrible at all. It was refreshing to be alone and have time to think." The interviewer asks which type of things Fenella read. "Oh, witch books, naturally, I needed to keep my hand in." She wonders if this is what happens when actresses act; they start out looking outward, seeing everything, but then hearing their own voice, turn into themselves, spin the story outward from something they've taken within themselves. This is what happens to Fenella when she is given free rein to speak, she loses her own mind and hears it told back to her. She loves it. This strange process! "I'm sorry, I didn't hear that one," Fenella says. The interviewer repeats the question. Fenella ponders. She answers carefully. She is actually interested in the answer.

"Witches aren't even people," Fenella says, sphinxlike. "Do I look like a person to you?"

I PREFER TO WORK ALONE," FENELLA SAYS, "GENERALLY, THANK YOU."

She keeps walking. With her head down so she can see the sidewalk, she doesn't know where she is on this sidewalk, she must watch it to see where it goes. She's wearing flats because it's easier to busily walk here and there in flats, her slightly gleaming ones, and a Swedish suit she's just bought. She saw it in the window of the store. *Like a modern ninja*, she thought and went in. The high collar of the wool-and-mohair-confected blazer is doing something to her neck below her ears, something unfriendly, like a burn, she tries to keep her head perfectly still to check the hot chafing. *My New York suit*, she thinks, so she can tell her sisters, this is my New York suit, and sound hoity-toity.

She doesn't really like New York. There are too many eastern witches, a northern one has to constantly be on the lookout, there is a conglomerate here. They try to absorb her. "Let me at least get you dinner," this one pleads, still keeping pace with Fenella, "or a coffee. We can talk about it at least."

Fenella keeps walking but considers the offer of a coffee. *It could be interesting*, she thinks, *it might be fun*, she looks sideways at the witch, he is not her age, not a soul mate, not anything recognizable to her at all, something new. *Something new*, she thinks, and her brain catches the brush of something fresh and sends out to her fingertips and limbs an unanswerable desire, she stops walking and turns to face him. The scarf tucked into her blazer flutters out and blows on a slight breeze. He looks at it, that is the thing that catches his eye, like his newness to her, and confirming what it is, a scarf in the wind, looks back along its length to Fenella's face. Absently, she catches the edges of her floating scarf and tucks them back into her jacket. "No," she decides. "No, I have never worked well with others."

"If you haven't worked before with the right people, you wouldn't know," he says.

"On my honor, it would be bad for you," Fenella tells him.

He becomes angry. Fenella stays still to watch. Anger like this is exciting and rare, she is a collector of it, she thinks, it collects around her.

"Do you think you did this alone?" he asks. "You think that you got here on your own? By yourself?"

"I never spoke a true word for help," Fenella says, "lady's honor, not one single word did cross my mouth, asking for help."

"That is not the point," he says. "You did not get here on your own. You owe a debt. You did not get here of your own volition. Alone would have brought you to a hill and a rope."

"Yes, so what?" Fenella says. "Maybe that is what I planned. Maybe you, and how you say you helped, did nothing but the opposite of that. Maybe I don't want to work with you because you don't know how to take direction."

He scoffs. "That is not what you planned," he tells her.

"Yes, and how do you know that for sure, though?" Fenella says back.

"I know."

"You don't even know me," says Fenella.

"Oh, I do," he assures her. "The question I'm wondering is do you know who I am?"

"Of course I do," Fenella answers, she's known all along. "You're that man from the Justice Department. You wrote me letters." Now he is a little flustered. "Of course I looked you up afterwards," Fenella tells him. "Your picture is on the website."

"Then you know all, everything, that I, that we have done for you, for you and for your purpose," he says.

"Yes, I know," Fenella says. She nods and holds out her hand for him to shake. "It's a pleasure to meet you in person," she says formally. He touches her fingers. "You don't have to be afraid of me," Fenella says.

He says, "I'm not afraid of you."

"But you can feel it, can't you?" she says.

He stares at where his fingers graze hers. "Feel what?"

"Not to come too close," she says.

He laughs. "I told them you would never stick to being called delusional," he says, "we had to spin it another way, that you knew what you were doing, but you are, you are a walking delusion, if you think you can keep this up, now, when we all know who and what you are."

"The world falls apart in a nightmare," Fenella says,

"and then you wake up and have to put it back together with broken pieces."

"What?"

"If you help again," she says, "I'll break the entire world this time instead of just mine." She smiles, she is being so highfalutin! Sometimes the occasion calls for it. Sometimes a little bit of theater is not misplaced. She tosses her hair. Now she is purebred lady. Something more familiar! She makes her fingertips flirt with his, his fingers on hers tense, drop away. "It was nice to meet you," Fenella says again. The wind blows her scarf up around her mouth. She holds it there, smiling through it. "Thank you for all the very kind letters you wrote to me." Her voice is muffled.

Whatever he hears, he hears and nods. "We'll speak later," he says.

"Yes," Fenella says, "for that coffee you promised me." She smiles brilliantly. She lets go of the scarf. It mingles through the air with her hair, he backs away from it, nods again; Fenella tips her chin to him, her high collar burns into the chapped skin, she winces, abstemiously, both she and he walk away from the other, she looks back, he doesn't.

Her soul mate comes back to taunt her. Now, after all this time, here he is again, coming through the library entrance exactly when she is here to see him come. She is out of her witch disguise of all black, she wears black-and-white silk stripes and fancy woolen trousers, and the silk blows in the wind from the door opening and closing behind them. *Extraordinary*, she thinks, *extraordinary*.

He's wearing sagging black sweatpants, untied black work boots, his dark hair's half in a sloppy ponytail. He looks like he's just gotten out of bed, or a garbage can. He walks straight past without looking at anyone, with a small smile to the floor. And what has the floor done to deserve it? She imagines his bed, the room his bed is in, the smell of it. The air floating around it and him like a galaxy.

She follows him with her eyes, her neck turns, she turns around and watches him, holding carefully to her pile of books. *What are the chances?* she thinks, and then thinks, *the chance is not so small*. Smaller if she had not seen him in the same place she saw him first, then maybe it would be a great chance, but this, she thinks sensibly, this is just two people coming to a place where they often come, at the same time. He goes into the elevator, this time heading up.

"I can help you now," the worker says. It's a lady this time, she sounds annoyed, Fenella's distraction is keeping her from important things. Fenella snaps back around. She will get this done quickly. She would like to get upstairs too.

She goes up to the desk and hoists her stack of books onto it. "These are all very late," she tells the lady crisply. She doesn't have time to waste. "I telephoned and talked to someone and they said you would be able to waive the fines if I showed you this." She takes her release papers out of her leather bag and unfolds them and flattens them out on top of the books. "There." She points to her incarceration dates. "See, I was unable to return them."

The lady looks sourly at the papers. "Well," she says, "I think I have to get my supervisor."

"Whatever," Fenella says. She looks behind her, she has been feeling, with her sensitive nerves, every person walking behind her, she can't let him leave today. Not today, this awesomely fortuitous day; not this day suddenly blown up with opportunity; not when he has swum into her hands will she release him.

The lady disappears into the back. Fenella turns around and leans against the desk, watching, dizzy. He doesn't come. This is good, he's lingering, she relaxes.

"Hello, Fenella, is it," comes a voice, and Fenella turns back around, the supervisor stands there with the sour lady. The supervisor has a familiar voice; she's who Fenella talked to on the telephone.

"Yes," Fenella says, "Yes, I'm Fenella."

"And you brought these in," the supervisor says, picking up and examining the documents. "Did you check them in yet?" she asks the lady. The lady shakes her head. "Then just go ahead and check them in exempt and we won't have to worry about paperwork," the supervisor says. She smiles at Fenella. Not phony. Just kind. "Anything else?" she asks Fenella as the sour lady pulls the books toward herself and begins checking them in.

"No, thank you," Fenella says, "that's all."

The supervisor hands Fenella's papers back to her. Fenella waits for the lady to finish checking in her books, there is no rush, he is safe upstairs, and she wants to make sure her account is clean because there's a book here she wants to take home. She folds her papers, she opens up her black-lacquered change box and puts them inside, drops the little box into her bag.

"So," the lady says, "what were you in jail for?"

"I was a witch," Fenella says, thinking it is very nosy of her to ask.

"You were a witch?" the lady asks. "Aren't you anymore?"

"No. That's why I'm here now. Can you please check my card, so I can be sure everything is cleared?" She hands over the library card. The worker scans it, looks to her computer, nods.

"Wonderful," Fenella says, now she can be polite again, "thank you so much."

She takes back the card and heads to the stairs. She measures her steps going up, watching the elevator: it will not do to have him go down when she is coming up. The sight line to the elevator fails and she skips up the rest of the way quickly.

In the stacks, the sound is dull. If he's in a study room, she's out of luck. She checks her breathing and slows her step. She mustn't frighten him. She goes up and down the center aisles, glancing into the rest of the rows. She can't find him. She turns around and walks through again. A lot of ugly, pointless people littering the place.

There is a quick, dark shimmering through shelves of books at the end of an aisle; she doubles back and swings into the aisle she's just passed as he comes walking down it toward the center, toward her. Keeping her eyes down she walks toward him. They meet, Fenella says "excuse me" to the floor, they pass. A subtle smell of black tobacco lingers in the air.

She watches after him. It is astonishing, seeing someone up close; everything changes, they become very human, very full and far away; there is a world behind him, right out of her sight. But now he is marked, now she will find him easily. For a moment longer, she stands there. Then, sedately, ladylike, she follows after.

ABOUT THE AUTHOR

Stefanie Moers lives in Minnesota and has worked in libraries for most of her life.

www.ingramcontent.com/pod-product-compliance
Lightning Source LLC
Chambersburg PA
CBHW070503170726
48291CB00008B/2635

* 9 7 8 1 9 4 8 5 5 9 3 7 9 *